# SON OF THE FORGIVEN

### A Novel

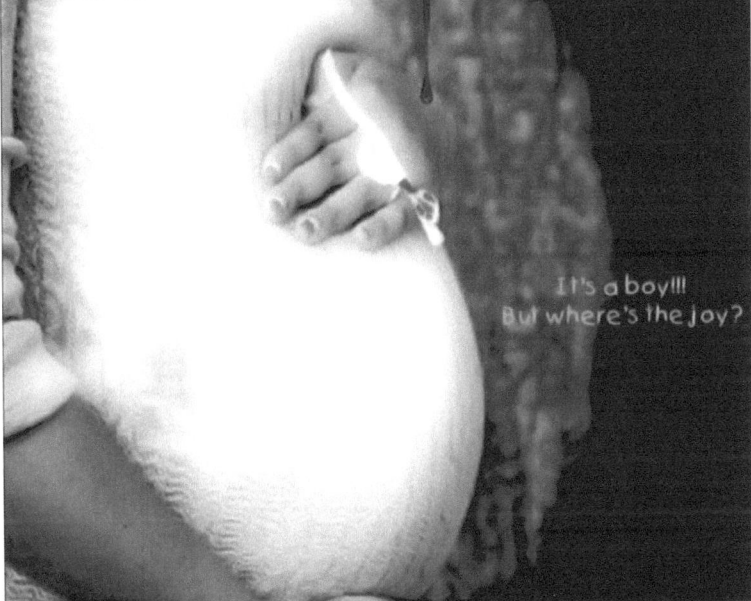

It's a boy!!!
But where's the joy?

## KIMBERLEY M. BYRD

# Son of the
# Forgiven

## Kimberley M. Byrd

# SON OF THE FORGIVEN

a novel by

## Kimberley M. Byrd

Word Eternal, Inc.

P.O. Box 625

Troy, AL 36081


Copyright © 2012 by Kimberley M. Byrd

ISBN: 978-0-9794433-1-2

Library of Congress Control Number: 2012941166


Author's photo by Brittany Britton

Cover Design by B. J. McClure & Que Creations

Cover Photo by Visual Memories Photography

Printed in the United States of America

## DEDICATION

This book is dedicated to all the sons of the forgiven in my life. First, to my daddy Albert McClure, thank you so much for the words of wisdom that you have spoken to me my entire life. I love you so much and owe my life to you.

Also, to my brothers Willie Albert, Randolph, James, and Greg, you are the four corners of strength that keeps me looking up.

To my nephews, Brandon, Shaun, Daniel, BJ, Juney June you all are too talented to ever visit mediocrity.

To my Godson Zachary don't ever stop doing, achieving and believing.

And a special thanks to little Christian Albert for always walking behind me asking, "Aunt Kim, you doing alright?"

Finally, to my husband, thank you for making my prayer life stronger. I love you with all of my heart even though we haven't met. My faith knows that you are an awesome man or at least you better be since you're making me wait so long. I'm trusting that God has released you to come find me.

# Acknowledgements

First, I would like to acknowledge that God is the head of my life. He is Sovereign, Supreme and the Giver of every good gift. I am appreciative of the gifts that He has entrusted me with. It is my prayer that I present them back to Him used to the highest capacity that He predestined.

As always, I am thankful to my mother, Pastelene McClure who has already gone on to be with the Lord. You motivated me to be the woman and writer that I am today and will evolve to be tomorrow.

Thank you, Eva Lou 'Grandma She-She' McNeal, for always having *Forbidden Fruit* on constant display beside your chair. I really appreciated your words of encouragement that you left with me before you went home to be with the Lord. Thanks Grandma for believing and speaking that I am going to make it. Your words shall manifest soon.

A great big thank you to my prayer partners, Diane Carter & Sandra Ikner. Without your effective fervent prayers I know I would not have gotten to this point. May God bless you Ephesians 3:20 style.

A huge thank you to Cornelia Briton, Janet Dempsey, and Shemekia McClure for being the proofreaders that really told me what I didn't know about having a baby. Your truthful insight throughout this project will always be valuable to me. I am most appreciative for you taking time out of your super busy schedules to help me out.

Lastly, but most definitely not least, thank you the readers for supporting me with your purchase. Thank all of you that have read my first novel *Forbidden Fruit*. I pray that I am giving you a brain teasing, rollercoaster ride of a story that keeps your interest from cover-to-cover. I write for you and because of you.

I had a lot of plans for my life but being saved, single, and pregnant wasn't one of them. Not once did the thought come anywhere even close to my mind. Marriage before the children had been my plan from the first day that I, Kenali King started liking boys.

Yet still, it's not so much the fact that I'm pregnant that bothers me. It's that the baby's father doesn't even know. That definitely wasn't in my plans.

It's funny how things work out sometimes. One minute I was calling fire down from Heaven and the next I was burning up with conviction. I guess this is one of those times when you can say that grace ran out but mercy endures forever.

But before you judge me, it wasn't as if I was a repeat offender that did what I wanted to regardless of how wrong that I knew the act was. Plain and simple; I fell to temptation—Once. My weakness was standing before me in a 6-foot-4, bald, reddish brown and handsome frame with a heart of gold. And just like gold in the furnace; I melted.

Yeah, I had been saved for a few years meaning that I should have been stronger than that but guess what; we all have our weaknesses. I often think back to that night and play it over and over in my head wondering if had I not been enwrapped in grief would the situation have been the same. Seventy-five percent of the time the answer is "no" but what about that small twenty-five percent. You know how the saying goes. If you give the devil an inch, he'll take a mile.

If I had to plead my case I would first start off with my track record. I had been abstinent for quite some time before the act that led to that fateful night. Actually to say some time is being mild and modest when in truth it had been years.

And yes, for those of you that are wondering, my last occurrence was with the same weakness. Yet he, Christian Jackson, was and still is just that. When I first got saved I actually pushed him out of my life since I was nowhere near strong enough to resist him. Years later when I needed him the most, at mama's funeral, he lovingly showed back up.

Anyway, back to pleading my case, when my mom suddenly passed away it rattled me to my core. Strength and calmness fled out the back door while fear tore in a new entrance, inviting some friends. I had never experienced anything like that in my life and never will again since there was only one woman that brought me into this world. I actually passed out for the first time in my life. Just hearing a few words that involved my mother no longer being on this earth floored me.

Not to mention, I was so afraid of losing my dad until I almost drove him insane with my constant calling and checking up on him. So, to give myself peace of mind I moved in with him for a little while. I'd say it was to give him some company and help him through this transition. But everyone knew the truth.

So to continue my case, we had buried my mom and just a few days later I conceived her grandchild while giving birth to a swelling river of tears. Some people may actually want to accuse Christian of taking advantage of me during my time of grief but I know him better than that. When it all boils down to it, I love him so much that like a mother who will defend her child with her very life, I will defend him especially now that he needs me to be a protector the most. And I know that questions are burning inside of you to know why he doesn't know about his child if he is such a remarkable individual.

That's the point where God's mercy endures forever comes in. In a week's time I had lost my mother, slipped in sin, got engaged to be married and almost lost Christian forever to a car crash. He cheated death by slipping into a coma recuperating until God says otherwise. And I also am careful to not say accident since I know in my heart that it was nowhere near that. If Christian could talk, he will probably tell that Julia intentionally drove the car over the edge of the cliff because she found out that we got engaged. Then again, all that devil in high heels had to hear was that he had just given his life to the Lord and she would have flipped out all the same.

I also had never planned on hating anyone but she just had a way with people that made it impossible not to. Julia was the weirdest case that I have ever met. Her strength in the wrong area was quite impeccable. And that's enough said about her since just the very thought of her sends chills up my spine and the heat of anger all over. I'm not that saved.

So, in essence, Julia's crazy love is why Christian doesn't have any knowledge of his child in which I had no knowledge of him either until morning sickness set in. At first, I had convinced myself that I was just under a lot of stress until I could no longer blind myself realizing that I was only stressed in the morning or when I ate something. Then to help matters even more, Divine, my oldest sister, knocked all the scales off my eyes by bluntly asking, "Kenali, are you pregnant?" It had to be the Holy Spirit telling her that or the fact that she has three boys. I had not told anyone of what had happened on that night and as far as I was concerned they could have just believed that I got pregnant like Mary.

Through it all, I can say like Paul, that God's grace is sufficient. I didn't lose my mind and I definitely didn't give up. Even when the doctors told me on two separate occasions that my baby had died in my womb, I looked the devil in the eye and told him he's a lie. My son is still kicking and doing well on the inside of me. That's just how much faith that I have. Even when I look down often at my engagement ring, I remember the promise that Christian made to me; we would become one. At the same time I remembered God will never leave nor forsake me. I am forgiven.

BEHOLD, I WAS SHAPEN IN INIQUITY;
AND IN SIN DID MY MOTHER CONCEIVE ME.

PSALMS 51:5

# CHAPTER 1

K enali stood staring out the window. She was looking more at her reflection than the trees or the birds that had previously caught her attention. Interestingly enough, her maternal figure became more gratifying than the changing of the seasons with the leaves starting to turn reddish-orange while the little red birds enjoyed their last few flights in the warmth of the atmosphere.

Indeed this reflection was more captivating than Mother Nature. Kenali was about to be the mother of this amazing little boy inside of her that fought so diligently to stay alive. In her mind, he was strong for the purpose of not bringing her anymore grief.

It was something spectacular about being showered by the glory of the sunrays that cascaded through the window. It almost felt like everything was going to be alright. She had faith that it would be despite those times that she felt like giving up. She had let go of replaying her mistake continuously in her mind. She just told herself to get over it for she wasn't the only one that had ever sinned. After all, she didn't want her baby to ever feel like he was a mistake. He was a gift from God.

This particular time out of the many, when she placed her hand on her stomach, absentmindedly caressing it, she felt as if her baby was praying for her. God knows that it took prayer to get her this far and it would take prayer from many to keep her. There were many nights that she cried herself to sleep asking God why she had to go through all of this. She never got an answer but just woke up in the morning feeling refreshed. She had been tried by the fire and strengthened by the power of the process.

Yet, today as her hands caressed her stomach, Kenali touched and agreed with the little one in her womb. Feeling so excited about the fact that soon she will be holding him in her arms, feeding him, changing his diapers, and doing whatever he needed to grow. She considered it minor chores for the way the baby was making her feel at this moment. Despite everything that Kenali had been through, not once had she blanketed him in the emotion of bitterness since that would be an admittance to defeat. If she lost it in this particular curve of her life then all the motivational words and speeches that she had given to others would be null and void.

Seeing her sister's reflection approaching, she turned her thoughts as her body did likewise.

"Hey, Baby Sis," Divine entered with greetings. Then Divine embraced her younger sister Kenali only pulling back to focus her attention on her increasingly growing stomach.

"It looks like you're going to deliver any day now."

"It feels like I'm going to deliver any day now. He's doing so much moving and kicking."

"That's a good sign especially with what the doctors have been trying to say. So have you decided on a name?"

"Yep! I sure have," Kenali beamed.

"Do I need to sit down for this?"

The two women burst into laughter for they both knew what Divine meant. She knew how her baby sister's personality was. There was no telling what she was going to name her first born once she sat down to allow her mental keys to start clicking.

"No, you don't. It's not eccentric," Kenali explained.

"Ok. Good. So what is it?" With anticipation, Divine clasped her hands together, entwined her fingers and rested her chin on them as she waited patiently to hear what name her sister had carefully plundered on for her soon-to-arrive son.

"He will be named after his father. His name will be David—"

"David!" Shock now replaced anticipation as Divine's eyes widened. "Who is David? Is there something that you need to tell me, Kenali?" Divine looked around to ensure that the chair was beneath her. As she reached for it she mumbled confirmation to her previous thought. "I knew I should've sat down."

"Girl, no. Christian's middle name is David."

"Oh! I'm relieved to hear that," Divine exhaled to release the shock. "All the years that Christian has been around, I never knew that. I just thought that your mind had slipped."

"Nope. My mind is still good. His full name is Christian *David* Jackson."

"I gotcha now. Just give me another moment to let my blood pressure regulate back to normal," Divine jokingly but happily explained.

Suppressing the immense grin that was trying to turn into a deeply belted laugh from seeing the shock on her sister's face, Kenali went on to finish naming her son.

"David Christian Jackson will be his name." Then Kenali paused momentarily as a question surfaced to her mind. "So do you think that if his name is turned around like that he'll still be legally considered a Jr.?"

Divine scratched her head looking to the air for an answer. "I don't know. But why are you turning his name around if I may ask?"

Everything on Kenali's face showed that she was elated to be asked that particular question. All the nights that she had thought on this very topic to come up with a perfected answer would be released finally to someone else.

"Because I have this feeling that when he's born, some things are going to turn around in my life through his little life," Kenali explained and prayed at the same time.

"Only you would come up with something like that." Divine happily smiled to know that her sister had not given up hope despite all that she had been through in such a short amount of time.

"Plus," Kenali excitedly continued, "I have to teach this little guy how to slay giants. Even though he may get in trouble or mess up, he has to keep seeking the embrace of God so much that He can't ignore him."

"Is that what his mommy did?"

"Yes it is. I let my guard down but my son is not a mistake. Christian and I love each other. Besides we are forgiven." Kenali's tone hushed as if to keep her unborn son from hearing her next words. "David should never be affected by what went on between the two of us."

"I understand where you're coming from. He won't know a thing about all the drama." Divine temporarily visited a personal place that was buried within. Then she shook it off to focus on now before she continued. "I can't wait to see his little bitty self. This is baby girl's first child. Daddy is so excited until it's ridiculous." Divine showed that she was equally as excited by the rising pitch of her voice.

"Oh really?" Kenali questioned with surprise.

"Girl, yes. You know how he doesn't let on about his emotions but anybody with eyes can see that he's happy on top of happy," Divine reassured Kenali with a smile.

"I just kind of felt like he was slightly disappointed in me for not being married," Kenali nervously bit her bottom lip while awaiting Divine's reply.

"Had you been a teenager, he probably would have been but you're in your thirties. You can take care of yourself and your baby. He doesn't have to worry about you struggling financially. And Daddy likes Christian. A lot!"

"Really? Thanks, Sis. I needed that."

"Besides, Dad is not a hypocrite."

Kenali was puzzled by Divine's comment. "What do you mean?"

"Do the math. Mom and Dad were married in June and I was born on Thanksgiving Day. Either I was three months premature or somebody had a bun in the oven already," Divine expressed with exaggerated facial expressions.

Kenali looked up as if she was calculating within her head. Then she gasped with widened eyes, "That's right! I really feel much better now."

Divine embraced her baby sister knowing that Kenali had been carrying around a great burden until that revelation came to her. She wished so much that she could protect her like she did when they both were younger but Divine knew that Kenali was at the age in which she had to defend herself.

"Well soon-to-be-mommy, I have to leave you now. I have to go to the office to check on some business."

"Alright then *Lady Di's Designs*. Thank you for stopping by and make sure you design something for your nephew. He'll be the only baby in the nursery with an original design on. From naked to designed. Now that's a line for Lady Di's

Designs," Kenali gave Divine two thumbs up with a cheesy smile.

"Girl, you're crazy. Let me get out of here," Divine giggled.

"See you later."

"Alright."

---

It was something about that visit that Divine had made with Kenali that was almost prophetic. A few hours later she went from looking like she was going to deliver any day to actually delivering today. Thinking back to the moment in the window she couldn't help but to wonder if that feeling was a natural way to let her know that it was time.

Kenali looked around at the doctor and nurses that were casually strolling around in a manner of comfort with their job. Then she couldn't help but to wonder why if they are the ones working why was she the only one showing signs of it. Never did she imagine that she would be one of the women that she saw on TV that were screaming out of control. At this point, she already knew that she and Eve were going to have a talk. Kenali hoped that she greatly enjoyed whatever fruit she accepted.

"I can't do this. Don't you have some drugs or something that can take away the pain?"

"Well Ms. King, you told me that you wanted to go natural to be healthier for the baby. And now it's too late to administer anything to you."

Even thou she was amidst a very great contraction having to deeply breathe like they taught her in Lemans class before she was able to speak, she had some hot words for that man.

"You're the doctor. So why would you listen to me?" She let out three quick bursts of air before continuing. "You knew I never had a baby before."

Even though she was now sweating profusely with tears rolling from her eyes, the doctor still let out a little snicker at her comment. Divine couldn't have come at a more perfect time.

"Kenali, you're about to have the baby," Divine exclaimed as she excitedly walked towards her baby sister who was in the position to give birth.

"Wow. Did you get a revelation or is it because my feet are in the air?"

Divine laughed out loud allowing the doctor and nurses that had been hearing Kenali's pain induced smart aleck remarks since the beginning to finally release a chuckle also.

"Why is everyone laughing at me? This is not funny," Kenali yelled out almost in tears.

Then one of the nurses came by to encourage her once more. "Like I told you before Sweetie, I've had four children and I know what you're going through."

Kenali dramatically paused. "If you knew what I was going through why on God's green earth would you do it three more times."

Although her sarcasm was on a roll, no one seemed to be bothered by it since they all knew that it wasn't a part of her usual characteristic. It was almost as if she was making their day brighter or something. She wasn't there in the gown of motivational speaker but she was in one that might as well have been on the floor since all her business was out in the open anyway. At this point she didn't care. The only thing that she wanted to know was why it had to be so much pain in giving birth.

"Divine," Kenali spoke quietly to her big sister who was wiping sweat from her forehead.

"Yes, Kenali."

"I think that I'm going to change his name."

"Oh really? To what?" Divine stopped wiping. She looked seriously into her sister's face to see what she had now concocted.

"Jabez. I understand why his mother said her baby brought her pain. I feel like I'm trying to push out an adult sized Jabez."

Now Divine, the doctor, and all the nurses released a laugh so great that they had to stop in place to release it. One of the nurses was squirming as if she was about to pee in her pants. But soon after they laughed, Kenali pushed for the last time. Then there was peace.

The pain was gone. There was silence. And although she had never had a baby before, her maternal sensors kicked in to alert her that something was wrong. She didn't know whether it was the fact that she didn't hear David's first cry or that Divine had the look of worry on her face as she watched the doctors and nurses that were once casually performing their jobs now break out into a rush and fuss over her little nephew.

Kenali's need to search Divine's eyes almost dared her to look to give her some answers.

"Divine?" Kenali had questionable worry in her voice.

"Everything is going to be ok," Divine robotically answered without even looking at Kenali.

And with that statement Kenali knew that everything was all wrong. She felt an overwhelming need to push again but not in the physical. In the spiritual realm she knew that she needed to pray until something happens. Everything had to be alright. David had been a part of her for almost nine months. There had developed a powerful love within her heart for him that she did not understand herself. They had been through too much for him to leave her now.

At this point, she began to pray that her baby live and be in good health even as his soul prospers which was the same prayer that she had been praying over Christian for all of these months. She had just become a mother and every instinct that came along with the territory rushed into her heart. Even before she heard David crying she knew that all is well.

The confirmation that prayer changes things hit her when they placed this beautiful little boy in her arms to catch the tears of joy that rolled down her face to fall into his. In a sense, she was baptizing him with the one thing that freely came from her heart.

Although there were other noises going on in the room the only thing that Kenali heard was the little sounds that came muffled under the breathe that now flows through his little body. This was one of those times that could not be a Kodak moment since all the emotions could not be captured by photography but it would be saved in her internal memory.

As she rubbed his full head of jet black hair, a smile came to her heart as she watched him try to open his eyes even though the light was too bright for him. Thinking to herself of how he came into this world fighting for his life just like his father has been doing the same, had to be the best example of like father like son that she knew of. As she held onto him, Kenali knew that everything was going to be well with the father and the son. Kenali just knew that little David's presence was going to turn things around. All eight pounds and twenty-one inches of him.

"Mommy loves you so much, sweetie."

# CHAPTER 2

"How's the new mommy doing?"

Kenali's sister Simbol entered into the room carrying the largest baby blue teddy bear that Kenali had ever seen. The two were almost equal in height. Simbol looked so excited to be a new auntie or perhaps that excitement was from her swiftly approaching wedding date to the man that was entering in the room behind her.

Kenali was always happy to see Lane, whose look yelled hardcore bad boy but never matched his true character. At least not the one Kenali had known all these years. Even when he was on the wrong side of the tracks, he was her biggest advocate. In fact, he was the largest contributing factor that led to her and Christian getting back together.

"I'm doing fine. How are the two of you doing? You look so happy and I have a feeling that it has nothing to do with me having a baby."

"Yes it does," Simbol interjected with school girl giggles floating on her voice. "I'm so happy to see that my baby sis has finally had her bundle of joy. Plus I heard that you acted the fool in the delivery room. You should really be ashamed of yourself. I so wished I could've been there."

"Yeah," Lane intervened, "they said that you were like a standup comedian but just lying down with your feet in the

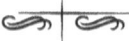

air." Lane leaned over to place a kiss gently on Kenali's forehead. Sincerely he asked, "Are you ok, Kenali?"

There was more to Lane's question than what was said. Kenali knew that he was referring to her having David without Christian being there.

"Yes. I'm doing fine, Lane. Thanks for asking. So have you seen Christian lately?" The question was asked with much hope on Kenali's part.

"It's been a while. I don't like looking at my cuz like that. I have to give it to you ladies. Y'all are a lot stronger than we are."

"We know. We just don't let you all know that we do. It might hurt your ego or something," Simbol sassily interjected.

"Ooops! Simbol, that's one of the things that you tell after the wedding or never at all. Speaking of which how's the wedding plans going?" Kenali perked up just from the thought.

Simbol's eyes brightened even more when the question entered her ears. "Wonderful now that you'll be back to your normal size. Girl, it was so hard trying to find a really cute maternity maid of honor dress. That's the real reason that we set the date that we did."

"Oh. I thought it was that you figured that we would be having a double wedding," Kenali said with a smile of hope on her face.

The room fell silent enough to hear a pin drop. Although Kenali was able to talk about the situation, Simbol and Lane still felt uncomfortable about it. Lane secretly hid his guilty feeling.

He was so happy when Christian told him that he was going to pop the question to Kenali that he wanted to tell her himself. For the short time that she proudly sported her engagement ring around, it was as if nothing could ever hurt her again. Then the accident happened. The ordinary person would have been crushed but not Kenali. She was like a different breed. Everything was happening to her back-to-back yet she was still standing beneath the grace of God. Lane often wondered if the tables were turned if he could overcome also. He didn't know. The streets were rough but this was heart issues which made them hard issues.

What he did know was that when his cousin did come out of that coma, he was going to have a strong woman there by his side for the rest of their lives.

Before he could finish his thoughts, Kenali started speaking.

"Look you guys; I don't want you to be saddened by when I talk about Christian. I love that man so much. Always have. Let me believe that he's still alive for the reason that he somehow knows that his son and I need him to pull through. Hope and faith is all that I have to hold on to. So believe with me. Let me talk about him. He's still here." Kenali sincerely looked back and forth between the couple that was standing on opposite sides of her bed.

"My sister is stronger than a ton of bricks." Simbol wrapped her arms tightly around Kenali's shoulders only releasing when she heard the nurse strolling David in to visit his mommy.

Pulling him up to the side of the bed and lifting him out of his crib to hand him to his mother, the nurse smiled as she positioned him in Kenali's arms.

"This little one said that he was ready to eat," the nurse playfully stated.

"Thank you," Kenali replied while looking down at her son the entire time.

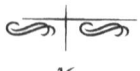

"I think he's real hungry. Is that him smacking that loud?" Lane questioned with disbelief in his voice.

"Oh my goodness! That's him making that noise. Is that natural?" Simbol turned her question of concern to the nurse who reassured that it was.

"Are you hungry? Kenali asked as if David could reply. "Tell your Uncle Lane if he could excuse you for just a moment while you eat."

"Go ahead and eat lil man." Then Lane looked around to find a chair and sat down. All three ladies looked at him wondering what he was doing.

"Sweetheart?" Simbol questioned in the most sincere voice that she owned.

"Yes," Lane answered.

"What are you doing?"

"I'm giving her time to feed the baby."

"She's about to breastfeed."

Lane's eyes increased. "Oh! I thought you were going to give him a bottle or something."

"This particular bottle is attached to the mommy and goes everywhere she goes," the nurse exclaimed as she headed towards the door smiling from his lack of knowledge.

"Sorry. I didn't think about the built in one. I don't have any kids," Lane was still apologetically explaining.

"It's ok Lane. When you and Simbol get married you'll learn it all piece by piece," Kenali said.

He smiled and waved to Kenali. "Simbol, just come get me when y'all are done."

"Will do," Simbol expressed with an unusually chipper tone.

Then Simbol was at awe looking at her new nephew for the first time.

"He's so beautiful, Kenali. I gotta give it to you. You and Christian made a handsome baby," Simbol whispered as if to not wake David.

As Kenali bared her breast to prepare to feed her hungry little offspring, she looked upon him with motherly admiration. Looking over him to see his father's characteristics, she smiled only to softly reply, "I know."

Once he was done eating, David drifted back off into a peaceful sleep in his mother's arms. After a while she passed him along to his Auntie Simbol who in turn moments later attempted to pass him over to Lane who had reentered the room. Out of fear of holding a small baby, he denied the pass.

"Why you don't want to hold my baby?" Kenali jokingly teased him.

"He's too little," Lane replied.

"He's a baby Lane. It's ok. You're not going to hurt him," Kenali reassured.

"Can I just wait until he's older? You know. Like three."

"You're going to wait three months before you hold David? What about when we have children? Are you going to wait that long also?" Simbol jumped in.

"Actually I was talking about three years."

The two sisters laughed at the sincerity and seriousness that was on his face. Lane was totally clueless about what was so funny but he managed to look past it to try to explain.

"Babies are so fragile that it feels like we will crush them. I bet you that Christian would act the same way."

Kenali briefly revisited the thoughts that she had many times before. In her mind she could see Christian nervously holding their son while she immediately walked into maternal awareness as soon as he was delivered.

"Sit right here Lane." Kenali patted to the side of the bed. She was going to give him his first lesson on holding a baby. She looked up to Lane as very trustworthy knowing that he would protect David with his own life just like Christian will.

"Now hold your arms like this while I place him." Kenali demonstrated before continuing. "It's a great experience Lane but holding David will not compare to the first time of when you hold your own."

Lane held his arms out like instructed revealing all of his tattoos on his forearms. A sleeping David was placed upon a large cross which now represented the new Lane while at the same time covering up something pertaining to his past street life. He looked down at David and then at Kenali when David began to readjust himself in Lane's arms. When he looked down again, two little eyes were trying to open to see who was holding him. At this moment, Lane felt as transformed as his body art.

"He's looking at me," Lane whispered excitedly.

From that point on, Kenali appreciated Lane even more. He gave her a glimpse of what it would be like when Christian woke up to hold their son for the first time. It was going to be an awesome spiritually bonding moment between the two men that she loved the most outside of her own father. She rejoiced to see the day.

Then as if her thoughts were read, her father came in bearing balloons, stuffed animals, and roses to the point that he almost needed a cart to carry it all but instead he had employed a parade of nurses following in behind him with more stuff in their hands.

"Daddy! What in the world would make you bring all this stuff?" Simbol asked as she walked to aid him in freeing up his arms.

"Seeing my youngest seed's seed," this proud grandfather explained.

"Who are you supposed to be? Father Abraham?" Simbol interjected with a smile and a helping hand.

"No. I'm Father King who believes in passing wisdom and blessings down through the generations. If I see to it that this little one is blessed then that means that I was a good man."

"Daddy, you're a good man already," Kenali expressed to her father as he reached down to hug her.

"You sounded like your mother when you said that."

"I wish mama could be here to hold David," Kenali spoke trying to not let sadness in.

"She held him first, baby girl."

Kenali's father looked down into David's face who was still nestled comfortably in Lane's arms. He began to rub his new grandson's head as if he was bestowing blessings upon him while trying to sense the spirit of his deceased wife. Then Lane offered David up to the arms of his grandfather, the man that he knew as Mr. King but David would know as Pawpaw just like the other grandkids had named him.

Seeing the transfer of her son from one man of strength to another made tears come to Kenali's eyes to know that her baby had no other choice but to be a good man as long as he was surrounded by such good examples.

By that time, Simbol who had been happily probing through the things that their daddy had brought finally broke out with a piece that greatly excited her.

"Awww Daddy, where did you get this shirt from? It is too cute." She held up a shirt that displayed the writing 'Grandma says I Can Do All Things Through Christ.'

"I had your sister make it. That was your mother's favorite scripture and answer to everything. It had been even since you kids were little. She was a really good woman you know."

To hold back the tears of everyone in the room, Kenali suggested that they put the t-shirt onto David now. Mr. King sat on the edge of the bed holding his precious grandson while Kenali gently placed the shirt over his head.

"The neck hole almost wasn't big enough, Daddy," Simbol cautiously yet comically interjected.

"Are you trying to say my baby has a big head?" Kenali came to defense of her first born.

"Well the apple doesn't fall far from the tree," Simbol replied.

"Don't make me put you out," Kenali sassily said with a smile.

"Do you remember the story that mama use to tell about the lady and her baby." Before Simbol could really finish what she was saying the two sisters and their father were laughing so hard. Lane of course felt left out. He was totally clueless at this point.

"What's so funny?" Lane asked.

"Well Lane, mama told us about this lady that had a baby. The word got around so much about the baby that people would be at the door stacked on top of each other trying to see the baby. Well the proud unsuspecting mother thought that everyone wanted to see her baby because she was pretty. The real deal was that people wanted to see the baby because the size of the baby's head," Simbol explained trying to keep her full laughter suppressed so that she could finish.

"That's one of the first stories that your mother told me when we were dating. At first I thought that she was incredibly shy but when she told me that, it broke the ice and I fell in love. Soon after, we were married and—"

"And then I arrived as the first born." Divine entered the room carrying some things for mother and child. "I could hear you all the way down the hall talking and laughing about the big head baby."

Then everyone fell out laughing again including Lane this time. It was such a happy atmosphere within this room. Lane was so proud to be about to walk into such a great family that received him so well despite who he used to be.

His mind reversed back to how he almost didn't want to ask Simbol out. At first he felt as if his past was not suitable for her. After Kenali and Christian insisted on setting them up, the rest was history. Simbol accepted him for who he is and not the street filled drug dealing man that he was. He now knew that God's grace was sufficient.

"So you two are getting a glimpse of how it will be when you get to this point," Divine broke into Lane's thoughts while crossing the room to hand Kenali something else that she designed for David.

"This is little designer gear for when he goes to see his daddy for the first time."

"Oh, Divine. It's so cute." Kenali was picturing how adorable David was going to look in his outfit.

"That's some nice gear. Do you make that in my size?" Lane joked.

"Sorry Lane. It's a one of a kind for my special nephew," Divine explained.

Simbol rewound her thoughts to when she would have been a mommy of two but abuse didn't allow that. She would often think about how if only she would have left that monster of a man that she was convinced loved her that the twins would be about three years old now.

To shake herself from that torment, she looked up at Lane to measure how happy he is to be here with her family.

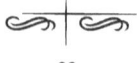

She immediately fast forwarded her thoughts to when they will get married with the possibility of having children. Thinking of a bright future with this good man made a warm inner grin replace the solemn look that she had on her face.

"I really wished I knew what just crawled through your mind." Lane hugged Simbol for her look showed that she greatly needed one.

Now completely smiling outwardly, Simbol was able to truthfully say, "Nothing. My focus is on the joy in this room."

"What are you two love birds over there whispering about? Don't worry. I'm going to make you one when you have your first child," Divine said.

"Well that time is coming very near. Lane, are you ready, son? Don't break my daughter's heart," Mr. King spoke with authority yet compassion.

"I won't sir. I'll do the best I can to make her happy," Lane honestly replied.

"Look at daddy, trying to threaten somebody. That's funny," Simbol lovingly joked with her dad.

"What's so funny about me having a man-to-man talk with my future son-in-law?"

"Nothing daddy. Nothing daddy. I was just playing around. Don't start flexing. You might hurt something. Then you'll be mad that you're downstairs in a room with a strained muscle."

"Don't let the age fool you. Your daddy still got it especially when it comes to my children's wellbeing."

"Speaking of wellbeing, it will be in Kenali and David's best interests if we let the two of them get some rest. So as big sis, I'm putting everybody out. Goodbye." Divine started escorting people to the door as if she was some kind of usher.

Everyone began to hug Kenali goodbye as they left the room. Even though Divine was the only other mother in the room, the rest of them could understand childbirth being a very taxing duty on the body including the little body that came through the womb into a big world that was all new to him.

# CHAPTER 3

"Look everybody! It's Kenali and the baby," one of the nurses exclaimed so loudly that you would have thought that there was an emergency. These are the nurses that have been taking care of Christian the entire time. They had become like friends to Kenali.

"Oh, bring him right over here so we can all get a look at the most anticipated baby of the year."

Although Kenali was anxious to go see Christian since it had been so long, she obediently placed David's carrier exactly where the nurse told her to atop the desk that she was sitting at in the nurses' station. An elderly man walking down the hallway with a cane in one hand and a rolling oxygen tank in the other, casually looked over their way partly wondering why she got to go behind the nurses' station while the other part could care less.

"He's so precious, Kenali," one nurse said it but all the nurses that were stacked on top of each other trying to see nodded in agreement.

"What is Mr. Handsome's name?"

"David Christian Jackson," Kenali beamed as she spoke his name.

"I know that the two of you are some proud parents. We're so glad that you brought him down to see us."

"Of course I was going to stop by here to let you all see him since we have been in each other's lives for almost a year. And you know that I'm just dying to see Christian also. He's in the same room right?"

The nurses looked around at each other in bewilderment and then back to Kenali.

"Why are you looking like that? What's wrong?" Kenali's heart was in her throat. Even if they did speak she would have to ask them to repeat it because of the loud heartbeat between her ears.

"Kenali. Christian is gone. You didn't know?"

Kenali was so shocked that she almost passed out. The only thing that she could do was to cover her mouth to keep from screaming. The nurses immediately pulled up one of the chairs so that she could sit down.

"What's wrong Kenali? We thought that would've been good news to you that he's no longer suffering in the coma. His nurse didn't call you to let you know."

"No one called to tell me that Christian had died," Kenali spoke through tears. She was so hurt that she had no clue of what to do next. This was a day that mimicked the one of which her own mother passed away.

"Kenali, Christian isn't dead. He woke up."

In the middle of one of the deepest sobs that she owned, her hearing alerted her to cease crying. Clarity was coming to her mind slowly but it was coming. She was thinking now, trying to put everything together to form a question.

"Wait. When you said that Christian is gone, you meant gone from the hospital?" Bracing herself, Kenali carefully waited for an answer.

"Yes. He woke up and was transported to another facility that had a Rehabilitation Center. He was doing very well but he was going to have to learn how to walk all over again."

"Oh really?" Kenali's tears had now been replaced by sheer excitement. She was bubbling on the inside. Something had told her that he was going to get up soon. "I'm just happy that he's out of the coma. We can take care of the walking part. Oh. When did he wake up?"

"Maybe a month or so ago. Shortly after you went onto bed rest," the nurses were now taking turns answering Kenali's questions that were coming at the speed of a mile a minute.

"So he would still be at the rehab," Kenali fired off.

"Yes. He's going to be there for a while. Maybe months unless he had someone that could be home with him around the clock. And with you having a new baby I would not advise that you take on that kind of responsibility."

"Ok. I have to get there. He's probably wondering why I haven't come to see him," Kenali sped through her words. The nurses were wondering if they needed to check her blood pressure.

Just as fast as her mouth was moving so were her thoughts. *Why hadn't anyone called her? Or more importantly, why hadn't Christian called her?*

"Slow down, Kenali."

"I'm sorry. I'm just excited. Everything is finally lining up." Kenali looked quickly at her engagement ring kissing it.

"That's right. Somebody is getting ready to go down the aisle. I hope that we can get an invitation."

"You know you will especially if you tell me how to get to where Christian is."

"I sure will. If I were on break, I would take you myself just to see this reunion of soul mates."

And the nurse was right. Kenali and Christian were a match made in heaven and now they were about to make eye contact again. He was going to be able to see the son that he had no knowledge of. That moment alone will be worth the long wait that she had to endure seeing him in a coma. She knew that David's birth was going to turn things around for her although she had to admit that she did not think that it was going to be this fast or this perfect.

As she drove to the other facility, she kept thinking of how life couldn't get any better than this while trying to avoid speeding. She couldn't say the same for her mind. If speeding of the mind was against the law, she would most certainly get a ticket. Her mind had so many questions with the main one being why Christian hadn't called her?

But as she focused her mind to think on more important things she caught a glimpse of the best one in the rearview mirror. He was so preciously fast asleep. Thinking or more so knowing that all because of David, God had changed things around right on time. Now her dreams will soon be complete. She will not only be the mother of Christian's son but also his blushing bride. For Kenali, things could not get any better than this.

# CHAPTER 4

While Kenali was on her way to see Christian, she reached for her cell to convey the good news to her sisters.

She decided to take a shortcut through a supposedly rough neighborhood without taking a second thought about it. Often she would come down to this area to work with the teens that had a desire to write but didn't think that they could make it due to their geography. She inspired them that they could do it but they must believe in themselves. Actually a few of them had gone on to become published authors which caused her to really reach out to more and more of the teens in this area regardless of how dangerous it was supposed to be.

Although she would not be stopping today, she scanned the area to see if she saw any familiar faces walking down the street. Then she thought about it being a school day and almost stopped her search for someone to blow and wave to when she saw a very familiar head of bushy curly hair. Not only was he out of school but he was so far from his home.

As Kenali pulled over, he spotted her. He knew her midnight black Cadillac CTS coupe from anyone else's even before he could see the black and silver tag on the front with *GOD IS GR8* imprinted on it.

As if he had no other choice, his body started to migrate towards her car.

"Hey Jamal," Kenali spoke calmly as if she didn't want to alert him that he was busted.

"Hey Auntie," Jamal tried to sound as normal as possible. On the inside, he knew that he was busted. He was really trying to scan her to see the degree of trouble. After spending all the time that he had with her, he knew her very well. Since she was the coolest auntie, he was hoping that she would just let him slide.

"Well I haven't seen you in a while. Did you get jealous because I got pregnant?"

"No. I've just been so busy."

"Too busy to come see your favorite Aunt and your cool new baby cousin. Now what could be that exciting?"

"You know I love you. Oh! Please don't tell Aunt Simbol that she's not my favorite aunt. I just kind of let her think that she is to spare her feelings. You know."

"Ok. I won't tell her but on one condition."

"What's that?" Jamal almost hated to ask.

"You tell me why you're not in school."

"Well…,"Jamal held onto that one word. He didn't know why he hadn't already thought of an excuse. There was no doubt that she was going to ask. Considering who he was talking to, an excuse outside the truth would have not been enough to stand up to her keen reasoning.

"Are you trying to think of something? Remember who you're talking to."

"Trust me. I already thought about that," Jamal's tone sounded slightly defeated.

"Young man, come on and tell me why you're out of school and why are you so far from home? Oh, and I can tell by your comfort level in your body language that you come here a lot."

"Aunt Kenali, these are people too. It just looks different from our side of the tracks but they're my friends."

"Oh I know that they are people just like we are. I came here all the time until I went on bed rest."

Jamal looked as if he was shocked to even think that his Aunt Kenali be hanging out in the hood. "What do you be doing down here? And why are you here now?"

"Well if you must know, I come here to mentor teens but today I'm taking a shortcut to see Christian?"

"I thought that he was in the hospital in the other direction?"

"He was. He woke up and was transported to a rehabilitation center on the other side of town." Just the thought was enough to stir up the many butterflies that were in her stomach.

"That's good Auntie! Now you can get married like you and mama talked about a thousand times. Oh and let me see my lil cousin real quick." Jamal sprinted around the car to the passenger's side. He opened the door, pulled the seat forward and hopped into the back seat in a fluid motion. "He's so cute. Hey lil dude, I just want you to know that you got you one cool mama."

"Yeah she so cool but she still didn't forget why her nephew is skipping school," Kenali added.

"It's been good talking to you lil cuz. I gotta go up here to talk to your mama now. I'll be coming by to see you a lot for the next two years in order for me to get out of trouble." After getting out of the back seat, Jamal immediately reappeared at the driver's side window ready to negotiate. "So what's it gonna be? Raking leaves or cleaning out the garage."

"You're so funny. Now answer the question so that I can figure it out. It may be both for three years."

Two pecan shaped eyes were looking at Jamal waiting for his lips to move with an answer to a question that he really had no answer. He just didn't want to go to school today. Jamal already knew that answer was not going to appease his aunt but it would have been the truth. The truth will set you free he thought as he just blurted it out.

"I just didn't feel like it today."

Kenali waited for him to say more but his lips stopped moving. After moments of awkward silence she realized that there wasn't more. She on the other hand had many words to say. After all, she was a writer with the ability to create some words. When she got finished with her long winded reason of why he should have been in school he will wish that he was.

"Jamal, baby, I love you and you know that education is one of the things that I really, really believe in. And that answer of just not wanting to go is not going to cut it. Besides, while you're here skipping school, what if something happened to you?"

"Nothing's gonna happen to me," Jamal whined.

"Where did you buy your crystal ball from?" Kenali shot back sarcastically.

Jamal sighed deeply as if he was tired of this conversation.

"Oh you tired of me talking? You'll be ok. I'm going to treat that one in the backseat the same way. Some people have parents who don't care anything about them but not you. You have parents and family that love you very much and they only want the best for you."

"Do they?" Jamal was getting dry in his response.

This was a side of him that Kenali was not accustomed to seeing. She partly attributed it to him being a teenager.

"Yes they do, Jamal," Kenali reassured him.

"Mama don't tell you everything," He stated while looking away towards his friends.

"What's that supposed to mean?"

"It is what it is auntie. People got secrets."

"That's true. They're entitled to keep their business to themselves if they choose. Just like I'm entitled to tell you to say goodbye to your friends and hop on in cause you going with me."

"Dang, auntie, please don't do me like that," Jamal whimpered while letting his head roll from side to side without restraint.

"It's not about staying on your good side. I'm trying to protect your back side."

Once again Jamal let out a sigh before giving in to her request.

"Aight. Hold up."

As Jamal ran off to say goodbye to the fellows, Kenali took her gaze from him to look in the rearview at her sleeping newborn. She could remember when Jamal was that size and how she loved him like her very own son. She always thought of him as a good kid always wishing for a son like him one day.

Divine and Gerald had done an amazing job raising him. It bothered her to think that Jamal thinks they don't care what's going on with him.

Then she glanced in the rearview mirror once more wondering if she and Christian will go through the same thing when David turned sixteen. Kenali smiled while she shook her head from side to side as if to erase anything dysfunctional that had been sketched in her mind.

"So I gotta go to rehab with you to see Uncle Christian?" Jamal asked while getting into the car.

"Yep!" Kenali gleefully exclaimed. Just hearing his name made her even more excited that he had awakened from the coma.

"You mean I gotta go through this mushy stuff?" Jamal sighed as if he was really serious but he had a smile on his face. He was glad that his auntie would finally be completely happy.

"Why do you say that it's going to be mushy?"

"Cause I already know. You can leave me and lil D.C. in the lobby. He's too young to be exposed to that kind of stuff."

"You know he has to come with me so he can see his daddy for the first time."

"Dude is going to be shocked. He might go back in the coma," Jamal joked.

"The devil is a lie," Kenali quickly counter attacked.

The auntie nephew duo cracked up laughing as they drove on to see Christian. Jamal always did know what to say to make her heart joyous. To hear him call Christian uncle was all it took. As a matter of fact, he was about to inherit two uncles from the same family cause now that Christian is awake Kenali is going to be hot on Simbol and Lane's wedding trail.

Yet and still, out of all the excitement of having prayers answered, there was a few aches nagging her heart. What was Jamal's real reason for being out of school? And most importantly why hadn't Christian called her?

# CHAPTER 5

The day was filled with such a romantic buzz. The air was sprinkled with the scent of Lavender from all of the beautiful flowers that had been brought in for this special day. People were busily making magic happen as they transformed this simple lake area into an enchanted garden that was fit for any one of royalty to wed in. If any couple deserved to get married it was this one that would unite in holy matrimony on this beautiful day.

As everything was professionally placed it did what was once thought to be impossible; it perfected nature. Kenali had hired the wedding coordinator Ardnas Renki. He came highly recommended as being one that brought tears of joy to every eye as well as openness to the mouth from seeing such awe.

Actually had she not seen it being done, Kenali would have wondered all day how he was able to make the sky rain this magnificent sheer lilac material which was speckled with a glittery substance to make it catch the sun's rays. It was almost as if the sun had come closer to the earth to shine over this space that led to the altar where vows will be swapped between two that will become one. Perfect.

And the altar was something that was very mystical. The pathway was clear so that it appeared that the wedding party would be walking on water. There was an amazing array of water fountains in the backdrop. At first the flower girl and ring bearer were a little fearful to walk upon it. Then after rehearsal the day before, they decided to lie on it looking into the water.

The pathway in the middle was the perfect width allowing the wedding dress to almost tickle the water without getting wet. Ardnas had added an extra romantic flair to the aisle for the bride and groom. He had covered the entire path with a thick layer of lilac and white colored flowers. Also he trimmed the pathways on the left and the right for the rest of the wedding party. The photographs were going to be amazing. Surely people were going to believe them to be Photoshopped.

Kenali then looked at her watch to see that the time was nearing for her to walk on water. As she turned to go inside with the other ladies to get dressed, she realized that her son had been conceived in a similar setting surrounded by nature although not touched by this many human hands. Before she could indulge any further into her thought, she heard her name coming from the forest. She leaned towards the direction that it came from to see Simbol ducking behind a tree.

"Why does it look like you're hiding in the trees?"

"I am," Simbol whispered.

"Why?"

"You know," Simbol responded no louder than the first time.

A puzzled Kenali answered back as she began to migrate toward Simbol who was apparently insistent on not revealing herself. "No. I don't know."

"If he sees me, it can be bad luck." Simbol looked around nervously.

"Oh. I'm glad that I'm not superstitious. Don't worry. You're about to become the blessed wife of Lane Jones."

Simbol's countenance changed as she dropped some of the weight. "You're right. I just don't want anything to happen to mess us up. I keep having a bad feeling that something is going to go wrong."

"Why? Because you're my sister?"

Simbol was so shocked at Kenali's statement. She wasn't even thinking about the things that had happened to Kenali. Simbol felt so guilty for she had not even thought about how Kenali would feel on today knowing that Christian was out there somewhere without a trace. She knew that Kenali was so crushed when she went to the rehab to find that Christian wasn't there either. The only explanation that they could offer her was that, "We can't force treatment on anybody. And we have no idea where he went after he left here."

Simbol noticed that after that day, Kenali shifted. It was as if everything that she believed or hoped for had been pulled from that spot in the middle of her that held everything together. And she had no idea how to help mend her back together again. So she kept encouraging her that everything was going to be alright regardless of how awkward it felt motivating Kenali.

To Simbol, it was like telling a billionaire that you were going to financially bless them by pulling a quarter out of your pocket to hand them; no affect whatsoever. Plain and simple, Kenali was the motivator that travelled the country motivating thousands. Surely she knew anything that Simbol would tell her. Yet and still, this is her sister and she had to attempt.

"Kenali, you know that I didn't mean it like that," Simbol sadly expressed.

"I know you didn't. Today we need to focus on getting you into that dress and out across that water. And I meant to tell you that I forgive you."

"Forgive me for what?"

"For making me wear a purple dress, a color that I vowed to never wear since Barney came onto the scene."

Snickering already, Simbol still had to find out why her silly sister had a vendetta against such an amazingly royal hue. "Girl, why?"

"I don't know. He just made purple look so round and big that I knew not to drape myself into it head to toe. Thankfully, I found a really good girdle to hold my mommy pooch in."

"You're so silly. Don't make me start crying out here. Do you know how long it took to do this makeup?"

---

As the couples walked down this enchanted aisle arm in arm, they each looked forward to walking across this magnificent display of man's creative thought manifested.

As Kenali walked down this aisle alone, she fought to not have that emotion display on her face. In all actuality, Kenali felt abandoned by Christian. It was as if he was running from her with the gap widening by the second. There were two insurmountable emotions fighting within her. There was the just give it up and go on about your life which felt awful but safe. Then there was the one that was the most gut wrenching; something is wrong so fight until the end.

Now she had to shake those thoughts from her mind to walk onto this platform without falling into the water. That would be a wedding blooper that no one would let her live down. "Kenali, do you remember when you went swimming at Simbol's wedding." Nope. She didn't want to go through that. With every step her mind became a little freer than in the step before. By the time that she reached her spot, Divine was halfway there. She once more wondered briefly if she and Christian had gotten married who Simbol would choose to be the Matron of Honor.

Today all the focus was on this beautiful bride that was on the arm of their daddy. Kenali first hand knew that their daddy was glad that he didn't have to walk out over the water. He almost applauded Ardnas when he stated the reason why Mr. King would pass his daughter over to Lane while they were still on land. He said that it marked the beginning of Lane and Simbol's new life together which was a journey only for the two of them.

At the minister's request, Mr. King passed his daughter's hand into that of a happily receptive Lane. Before letting their hands go, her father placed a kiss of blessings ever so gently on her forehead while he covered both of their hands with his. Simbol's heart warmed enough to let a tear spill from her eye. Divine and Kenali mirrored her action as they composed themselves enough to direct the flower girl to come to them and the ring bearer to go over to the man that replaced Christian as best man.

The couple began to walk on the lilac petal lined glass platform which in some spots had been doubly anointed by the cutest little flower girl who had been persistent to stop and sprinkle every spot with care despite the nervous ring bearer's obvious show that he wanted to get this over.

All the congregants looked in amazement. This was a sight for anyone to behold. The more this couple walked the more the train of her dress followed so gracefully behind. This dress was an amazing display of tailored talent which pieced together a chiffon fabric so white it was as if it were made from the plushest clouds.

Even when they were little girls, they would lay on the ground looking up to the sky to name the shapes that these types of clouds formed. Not once did they ever see a wedding dress.

Now standing here in front of the minister and adorned in the beauty of this white dress with a lavender outline that came around her waist to descend to the mini cathedral train, Simbol was convinced that she deserved to have her dreams come true. She placed a thankful look over to her sisters who were both holding back tears the best that they could. Divine being the oldest and the closest in proximity to Simbol wanted to reach out to hug her but reframed from doing so. The certainty level was high that they would fill this body of water that they were standing over with tears of joy.

Then Simbol looked at Lane with eyes filled with love, grace, and gratitude. She was so thankful of how Lane didn't treat her. She had been in an abusive relationship in which daily she was verbally abused that more times too many became physical. Now here she stands today with Lane, a lover of God, and a good man that she will cherish as long as God gives her breath in her body.

Before she knew it, they had been pronounced before everyone as Mr. and Mrs. Lane Jones. Simbol felt so high that she didn't ever think she could or would want to come down. She wanted to be like the fountains that was all around; constantly flowing without end. She felt this was a good day to be alive. Today she was going to live happily ever after.

# CHAPTER 6

N
ow that all the festivities of the wedding were over and the newlyweds were enjoying their honeymoon, Kenali could now sit back to think of plan B. Everything was happening so fast. With all the responsibilities of a newborn, Kenali truly didn't know what to do or even if she should do anything. After all, her time belonged to David now, who was fast asleep in his crib.

After not seeing Christian twice in one day was insurmountably disappointing. That just wasn't a good day. As she walked out of that rehab without seeing Christian her heart cracked.

Kenali felt as if she had made the worst mistake in her life back accepting him back. Now she had his baby and he was running away from her. How could he do that? Or even better, why is he doing this? Kenali's insides were in a tug-o-war just from the thought. She was torn between the one side that said suck it up accepting that he left and the other that said fight for him this time.

Then as if she was so full, her words began to spill to her lips.

"Maybe this is what's best. What if this is God's way of telling me that we're not supposed to be together?"

Kenali's eyes began to burn as they were seasoned by the saltiness of the bitter tears of rejection. As they began to flow down from the outer corners of her eyes, she cupped her hands over her face to really keep from screaming out. There was too much exiting her spirit at one time for her to handle. Never until now did the thought cross her mind that she and Christian were not intended to spend the rest of their lives together. The thought that he was just there to help her through the grief of losing her mother made her grieve all the more. If her mother was here, she would know exactly how to counsel her heavy hearted daughter.

"Oh mama, I really need you." She desperately cried out.

Too much too soon caused Kenali to buckle over in the oversized plush chair where she once peacefully sat with her feet underneath her. Now the weight of her heart declared that her chest meet her knees as she transformed into the fetal position. Although her mind was still in turmoil, it felt comforting to ball up like this. And for the first time in a long time if ever at all, Kenali cried in defeat.

Then as if to break her from this train wreck of thinking, beautiful sounds began to come from her son's crib. They were sounds of playful cooing. As she migrated his way, wiping her face, she exhaled. Now standing over her still sleeping son, she sees that he is smiling almost laughing. She remembered what her mother said about newborn babies smiling and laughing. Her mother had said that they were playing with the angels. Kenali joked with her by saying that they probably had gas.

Right now, she was holding on to the angel theory. She hoped that this angel was sent by God to cover her son so that he will not be tainted by the fears of his mother. With that thought something filled Kenali with a new strength. Now she knew that she had to fight like never before.

"Don't worry, sweetie. Mama is going to find your daddy and bring him home."

Now Kenali's spirit was lining up with her newly spoken words which were a lot better than before. She felt a more dominating feeling come upon her that stated that everything surrounding Christian's disappearance was not sent by God but had an ugly hand that was designed to crush her. Looking at David, she knew that the stakes were higher now. She had become powered up. As she turned to walk to her computer she spoke a testimony to herself while speaking defeat to those negative feelings that tried to overtake her.

"I beat you before and I'll do it again."

# CHAPTER 7

"Where's this boy at?" Divine looked at the clock on the face of her cell phone when she hung up from another failed attempt to reach Jamal. It was 2:46a.m. She didn't have the gut wrenching feeling that something was wrong. He was just acting out. He had been acting like this in one form or another ever since the day that he found the letter.

He wasn't even supposed to be home from school at that time. Divine blamed herself for leaving it on the couch although she couldn't help but to lose all self-control after reading the words. Divine was so frightened when she was glancing over the mail and saw the correctional facility stamp on the envelope. It was not a wrong delivery. It was her name on the outside of the letter. Then she turned it over on the back debating on opening it. In its blankness she saw the movie that caused her fear.

Every detail of sixteen years ago flooded her mind. She and Gerald were engaged at the time. Happily she was out shopping for a wedding dress. Divine was supposed to be meeting her maid of honor one day late in the evening after work but for some reason missed the call that she wasn't going to be able to make it.

So while she sat in her car waiting, a man came up tapping on the window. Even though he looked friendly, Divine only cracked the window just a little. He was saying that he needed some help because he had locked the car door with his child and keys in the car. Divine panicked. She remembered the forwarded e-mail that she thought was just a hoax to attempt to scare people or make them aware.

When he put the barrel of the gun through the crack of the window, all her ability to function left her; Divine saw death in 3-D. She unlocked the door as he commanded. Maybe it was just a carjacking she thought until he made her climb over to the other seat. If the gun had not been on her mixed with legs that felt like jelly, Divine probably could have jumped out the passenger side to make a sprint to safety. She felt hopeless as the car sped from the parking lot with the gun pressed heavily into her side.

Then after he got her to the wooded area that he had already predestined to bring some scared helpless victim, he began to rip her clothes but now she decided to fight. She made up in her mind that she wasn't going out that easy. Suddenly Divine felt her body go limp when he hit her in the head with the butt of the gun. And although she wasn't unconscious she was in between that and the other being able to realize everything that was going on.

Divine was overcast by a numb paralyzing feeling that froze any attempt to struggle anymore. When this horrible man was done, she felt relieved that he would just leave her there until she heard four shots being fired from the gun. As her body twitched she became aware that she was the intended target. Then he peered in to look at her to see if she was dead. She stilled herself to give him confirmation.

Hearing a truck crank, Divine knew that he had already been there planning it all. She was glad that she resisted the urge to begin the crawl to her car. The speeding truck was coming towards her. From the sound of the bass of the truck it was either old or had muffler problems. Feeling the wind and dust that had been sent her way by this speeding truck, she was thankful that he didn't run over her head which was only inches away from his tire. The truck had a distinctive smell. It was definitely old.

Divine never knew how she made it to the hospital. The last thing she remembered was dragging her bullet filled, bloody, violated body to the car with much agony.

Before opening the letter, her mind continued to flash back this time coming to the courtroom scene where her stomach was full of the seed that this criminal had left. He looked at her as if he was shocked; almost irritated that she didn't die. Divine was the only survivor out of five victims. She was the ghost that was full of the DNA that hung him.

Death row had been his home for sixteen years and now this letter had to show up confirming her fears that he did know where she lived. Her heart pounded harder at the idea that one day he could break out to come finish the job. Those were the words that he violently threatened her with as the officers forcefully removed him from the courtroom. She prayed almost every day since then that he found his way to the electric chair before he found her.

Now it was 3:30a.m. on the dot when a car pulls in front of the house. Jamal casually gets out. She sat in the living room waiting for him to get into the house. His body language showed that he was either not aware of the time or just didn't care. Divine on the other hand was going to let him know that he needs to snap out of it.

"Jamal, I have been calling you. You had me worried sick." She sniffed him lightly since he reeked of alcohol. "Have you been drinking? You need to answer me. Where have you been?"

"Out," Jamal said struggling to stand to control his swaying, drunken body.

"Out?!" Divine paused. Surely she knew that more had to be coming. After the awkward silence, she continued. "Let me tell you something young man, one word isn't going to cut it when it is almost four in the morning and you're just strolling in here drunk!" The pitch of her voice increased. "You better be glad that your father isn't here to see you come in like this."

"That would be impossible." Jamal's words were coming out slowly.

"Son, I know your father works a lot but he's going to dayshift as soon as he finishes training his replacement. He works hard to support us. Not support you in drinking."

"My father didn't choose a shift, he chose a death sentence."

Oh my God Divine's spirit cried out. Why did he have to find that letter? Divine softened.

"Gerald is your father. He doesn't see you as anything other than his son." Divine struggled to say it through the tears in her throat. Jamal was forcing her to explain through her pain.

"But I'm not. I always felt like I didn't fit in this family anyway. I knew something was wrong! True. It was convenient that Mr. Gerald was white like that man. But I always wondered about my eye and hair color." Jamal's anger was escalating.

He was surrounded by confusion like bees to honey. This had been growing inside of him since he found the letter, eating away at him like cancer. He didn't know how to handle it. He felt alone; trapped almost.

"Jamal, you have to understand that we love all three of you the same. You are no different than—"

"Yes I am! I am the son of a rapist and a murderer," Jamal shouted. "I didn't come from love like Chris and Nick.

I would've never been here if that didn't happen. Why didn't you do us both a favor and just had an abortion?"

Tears began to come down Jamal's face as he turned away from her to climb the stairs. Then she grabbed his arm when all he wanted was to go hide in his room. He got so frustrated that he pushed her down although he never meant to.

Then salt was added to injury as he tried to reach for her. Divine drew away in fear. He didn't realize that what she saw was the man on the night that she was attacked. Jamal had such a large resemblance to his biological father despite her prayers that Jamal would look like her. Divine loved her son greatly but she feared that look in his eyes. These were the same greenish brown eyes that she loved to see. Tonight they brought chills to her spine.

Jamal fled out the door into the streets that had been calling him from his blood. While he ran, he wanted to run out of existence. He felt like a criminal. How could he have pushed his mom down like that? But what was even worse was how could she be afraid of him? The fear in her eyes was the confirmation that he needed to know that she didn't really love him. So he fled deeper into the world in search of a place to call home for he would never return there again.

# CHAPTER 8

"Honey, this is so beautiful," Simbol exclaimed. The view was breath taking. The water was a serene blue that had to be a mix of water colors. It beautifully toyed with the white sands of the beach.

"It is," Lane replied with the same sentiment.

The newlyweds agreed as they watched an awesome sunset. The sun looked like an oversized orange beach ball that had been allowed to drift at the mercy of the ocean.

Although to have a ball that size one would have to be a giant. In the eyes of Simbol, many giants had fallen in her life the very moment that she said "I do." She never thought that she could ever be this happy. No. Never.

As Simbol sat quietly holding her husband's hand, she used the other to secretly wipe away a tear that formed behind her dark sunglasses. She remembered the last time that she had sat on a beach. It was a few years ago when her mom had to force her to go to Jamaica with the entire family.

Back then her mind was so controlled by that beast of a man that she was desperately in love with. Her mother tried so hard to get Simbol to believe that she deserved better. Yet in her mind he was a pretty good guy who just needed to release a little frustration every now and then.

He was even frustrated that she went on the trip and her family wouldn't pay his way also. Disrespectful is what he called it as he slapped her around making such a peaceful trip not really worth it at all.

It would be two more years before she would wake up to painfully understand that he didn't love her. She was so happy to be carrying twins. Every day she now had a reason to get up to live life. Plus due to the fact that she was pregnant he was less frustrated until one day he felt disrespected once again.

While in the mall, a completely strange man hurriedly trailed his toddler son whom had reached her stomach to simply say, "baby". This strange father who apologized to them for his son's sprint to her simply said as he was leaving with his son's hand in his, "Congratulations. I know you're going to make an excellent mommy." The man gave a friendly smile before disappearing into the crowd of people.

Simbol never knew what her live in boyfriend heard in his psychotic mind but by the time that they reached the house he was a new form of angry called thirty-eight hot. Even though he didn't threaten her by pointing his gun at her this time, he reloaded the clip of his fists.

By the time that she reached the bottom of the stairs that he angrily pushed her down, she knew that she had injured something internally. He didn't even come to the hospital this time to see what she had to; two little bodies that didn't survive the fall. All they needed were two more months before they would be here.

Simbol wanted to die. Happiness was ripped from her womb. He was going to pay severely. This time she told the police exactly what had happened. It was not an accident. She did not slip and fall. She didn't bump into the cabinet. It was all him as she gave his full name. She wanted him to lay in a grave like these two little boys that would never run around to pull on her skirt tail crying out "mommy".

No. Never did she think that she would be able to trust another man to not only enter into her life but to marry.

Before they got to this point she had secretly compared Lane against the beast of her past. She wanted to see if there was any hidden resemblance. No longer would she be quick to trust her own judgment of character but felt comfortable knowing that Lane came highly recommended from Christian and Kenali. Just thinking of this couple, she prayed within her spirit that they would soon find their happy time together on the beach as newlyweds.

"I'm jealous," Lane said.

"Of what?" Simbol questioned as she jolted from her thoughts.

"The thoughts that are holding Mrs. Jones more than me." Still holding her hand, Lane sat up to hover over her reclined body. "Baby, it seems like you're millions of miles away from here."

"I was just thinking about Kenali and Christian's struggle to be together," Simbol stated half of the truth. She had only hinted to Lane about her past that she so desperately wanted to conceal.

"I don't know how or when but they're going to be ok," Lane reassured her.

"I know. I just don't understand why or how a man that has to learn how to walk all over can just walk away without a trace." Simbol's eyebrows wrinkled into a tight frown.

"I don't like that either. Something's telling me that this is foul. I had already made up in my mind that as soon as we get back, I'm going to find my cuz. He has a special family that needs him."

"Oh. So you weren't going to tell me what you were going to do?" Simbol slightly joked around with Lane.

"I mean I was but after we got off our honeymoon. Cause right now me and Mrs. Jones got a thing going on." Lane tried to sing the well know song that was a perfect fit to this conversation.

While he continued to hold her hand he pulled her forward so that he could straddle the lounger behind her allowing her to lean back onto him. He wrapped his arms around his new wife cleaving to her while trying to signify to her that she was safe with him.

He did remember years ago that Christian had told him what happened to her. All the street that was in him searched for that man. Lane was going to make that beast pay for what he had done to the woman that he had a hidden desire for. Unfortunately, the police found him before he did.

Now as they sat as the perfect newlyweds, he already knew that he was going to have to be forgiven for the things that her past did to her. She was well worth him humbling himself to apologize for things that he didn't do.

And if Christian and Kenali were on her mind, then he was going to do everything in his power to make it happen. Simbol deserved that and so much more.

# CHAPTER 9

"Oh Kenali, I just don't know what I've done." Divine cried into her hands that had her face completely covered.

"He was going to find out the truth one day," Kenali reassured. She rubbed Divine's back in a very soothing motion just as she did David when he was fussy.

"But you don't understand Kenali. I drew back from my own son in fear. It was something about his eyes that looked like that man. I was so afraid." Divine cried just from the thought. "I know that I made the situation worse by doing that. But I couldn't help it. Then I saw the hurt in his eyes before he ran out the door. What kind of mother am I?" Tears flowed heavily from Divine soaking the top of her shirt.

"You're a great mother that has had something horrible happen to you but prevailed against it. If you can survive that night then you can make it through anything."

Kenali silenced herself to listen to her sister's sobs as she held onto her rocking back and forth. She didn't know what else to say.

"And that's just it Kenali. Only my body survived that night."

The tears really began to flow from both sets of eyes. Kenali searched inwardly for something motivating to give Divine but that gift failed her at this moment. She almost felt guilty for a slight release of something that had been building up inside of her since Christian's disappearance. The shedding of tears was doing them both some good. Then just like that, something very helpful came to Kenali.

"I think I may know where Jamal is."

Hope dwelt on the face of them both.

"Where? Let's call Gerald to tell him to go by there too. We have to find him before he does something crazy," Divine said desperately.

"No. Let Gerald keep his search going. I have to go there myself."

"Lord, please let him be there. Bring him home Kenali. Please bring my son home. Be sure to tell him that I love him so much," Divine pleaded.

"I will. Do you mind keeping David?"

"No. I don't mind. He brings me joy whenever I'm around him."

"Ok. Thanks."

"No. Thank you."

The two sisters hugged before Kenali grabbed for her keys and purse. As she was headed out the door, she gave Divine some final instructions for how to care for David.

"At 10 o'clock give him this medicine before he eats. It keeps his seizures under control." Kenali placed the medicine into Divine's hands then kissed David with prayerful lips that he doesn't have one ever again. It made her so afraid when his little body would shake uncontrollably like it did. She was consistently giving him the medicine which greatly reduced his episodes.

"Don't worry Kenali. I'll take good care of your son. I love you sis and be careful."

"Love you too and I will."

As Kenali walked the streets where she saw Jamal at on the day he was skipping school, she didn't recognize a single person until she heard a familiar voice call her name.

"Hey, Ms. Kenali."

Kenali turned to see the face that matched the voice.

"Hey, sweetie. How are you doing?"

She embraced Shakenda, one of the teens that she had been mentoring before she went onto bed rest.

"I'm good," Shakenda replied with a smile.

"Have you been writing?"

"Yes and no." A smirk crept onto Shakenda's shy face that had been hardened slightly by having to mature before time.

"Good on the yes. Now what's the reason for the no?" Kenali smirked back at her.

"I had writer's block."

"Writer's block? Girl, what's his name?"

"How do you know it's a boy? Are you having me followed?" Shakenda giggled and blushed.

She missed talking with Kenali. She always felt like she could tell her anything without being judged. Kenali was like the big sister that she never had.

"I have eyes in the back of my head remember. It's ok to be in puppy love but don't throw away everything for him. Understand?" Kenali's tone changed from being playful to serious. She really wanted Shakenda to do something great with her life.

"Yes ma'am. I won't. When are you going to start coming back to the center? We miss you."

"I miss you too. I'll be back soon. You know that I gotta show you my lil poopie," Kenali beamed.

"Oh yeah, Ms. Kenali, you aren't pregnant anymore. A boy or girl?"

"A boy."

"Do you have a pic?"

"Of course!" Kenali had plenty of pictures of her baby. She swiped the screen of her cellphone. When she looked through the gallery, there were numerous pictures that she wanted to share but it was one that made her heart melt. She glanced with warmth in her eyes before turning to let Shakenda take a look.

Shakenda held the phone with soft excitement. It was as if she was holding the baby being careful to not squeeze him too hard.

"OMG! He is so cute." Shakenda continued making goo-goo eyes at the screen of Kenali's phone.

"Thank you so much," Kenali paused weighing if it was the right time. "And I have another pic but it's not of my little one. It's of another young man that is very special to me. I hope that you can help me find him."

"I'll do anything to help you out. Let me see so I can spread the word."

Shakenda was really hoping that she had seen him. She wanted to help Kenali find anyone that was important enough for her to leave her baby to come find. Kenali turned the phone back to her with another picture. This time is was Jamal. Shakenda received the phone back again looking quickly.

"Sorry, but I haven't seen him around here. If I do, I'll be sure to give you a buzz."

Kenali was slightly disappointed. She was sure that he would be here but she didn't give up hope.

"Thanks. He's my nephew Jamal. And I don't get an OMG he's cute response for him. Probably cause he's not a baby hunh?" Kenali smiled with a blush being returned to her. "Oh. You do think he's cute. Look at you blushing."

"Ms. Kenali, stop." Shakenda was trying her best to not go into a full school girl grin.

"Maybe I can introduce the two of you if I can find him. You're about the same age, he's tall and I think you both would be cute together. I mean that is if writer's block isn't a serious thing."

Still blushing, Shakenda looked away. Kenali's cupid ability had flared up once again. She wasn't the kind that just hooked anybody up but she was fond of this young lady. After all, this was her nephew that she was talking about who was like her son so Shakenda had to be real special for Kenali to even attempt.

But what made Shakenda blush wasn't the mentioning of a boy but that she had just lied to her mentor. This was the same woman that made her realize that she can be anything that she put her mind to. So why did she not tell her that she had seen her nephew?

"So what made you look for him here?" Shakenda said trying to sound as normal as possible all the while hoping that her lying tongue would not be discovered. She couldn't bust Jamal since he probably needed some time especially with the way he was acting.

"I saw him down here shortly after I had the baby. He was hanging out while skipping school. So I just thought that I would give it a try."

Shakenda could breathe better knowing that she had not been discovered.

"I'm not being nosey but I am. What did he do?"

"Nothing really. It's just a big misunderstanding and his mom is all worried about his whereabouts. That's all."

"Oh ok. Well I think I better get back to the house before mama be tripping too. If I see him along the way, I'll holla at him about going home."

"Thank you so much. Do you want me to drop you off?"

Shakenda tensed up at the thought of Jamal standing outside of her place when they pulled up. "Oh no. It's just right over there. Thanks."

"Ok. Take care of yourself. And see you soon."

"Bye."

While she hurried home to go alert Jamal that his aunt was looking for him she wondered why he never mentioned that's who he was related to. Was he ashamed of her because of where she lived? It had to be something. Jamal knew that she was passionate about writing so why not mention that your aunt is a writer.

Those were the exact words she asked him in a baby soft voice. The change in voice was coerced by him being in rare form today. He was very different in a weird way when he showed up early that morning tapping on her window.

"Why you never told me that Ms. Kenali was your aunt? She's my mentor."

Jamal answered without moving from his stare. The shrug of his shoulders appeared to have made his lips move.

"I don't know."

"And what's going on anyway? You acting real funny today," Shakenda asked in hopes that he would tell her something.

Still answering from his daze, he simply said, "Nothing. My head is just banging."

"That would be the result of getting drunk. I don't know why you hang around them clowns anyway. They're no good." Shakenda paused to take note of his body language before she continued. "Look Jamal, all I know is that your aunt is looking for you. And *nothing* didn't get her to come down here flashing your picture."

Those words had the ability to make him move. Jamal sat up straight from his reclining gapped leg slouch that once held him. Looking into her eyes, he searched for the entire scene.

"When was she here?"

"Just now. And she said she was about to ride around looking for you."

"You didn't tell her that I was here did you?"

"No. Your secret is safe with me."

"Ok. Good."

Shakenda desperately wanted to know what was going on. Maybe she should have told Kenali that he was at her mom's apartment. Kenali probably could have helped him a lot better than she could. Shakenda hasn't really been able to reach him for a few weeks now. His whole personality had changed. He was now reckless and she was afraid of what he might do to himself.

She just had to know what was going on. Before she could ask, Jamal made his new plans known.

"I'm gonna go find my auntie. Knowing her she'll knock on every door like the po po until she finds me. I don't want her to knock on the wrong door."

"Are you coming back?"

"I don't know. I just need to clear my head."

"Why won't you tell me what happened?" Shakenda made another attempt.

"I don't know." Jamal released a deep sigh since all the uncertainty was surrounding him.

"If you don't want to talk about it, that's cool." Shakenda felt that she needed to back off. She didn't want to push him away from her and into the hands of more of the wrong people.

"I appreciate it," Jamal continued to speak in a grave tone.

"And you can come back if you want to."

"Alright but I don't want to get you in any trouble."

"My mom won't be home until this evening."

"Ok. I might come back. It depends on how it goes down with my auntie."

"Ok. See ya later."

"See ya."

Jamal's turning to walk out of the door was almost forced. He didn't want to leave the peace that Shakenda offered. He liked her style. She wasn't typically the nagging type until she met his aunt today. Although he knew that he couldn't hide out there forever he did appreciate her letting him sit there for these few hours.

Now he had to go find his auntie that was determined to save the world. He didn't want her to knock on the door of someone that had the same mindset of his real father.

Jamal couldn't have rounded the corner at a more perfect time. She was surrounded by two wolves that had hungry looks in their eyes. Anger flared up within him partly because he desperately hated the blood that ran through his veins while the other part was thinking about something happening to the people he loved.

"Woman, why are you down here looking for me?" Jamal shouted out startling everyone especially the man that had his back turned to him.

"Dang, young blood, don't be running up on nobody like that. I'm glad that she was looking for you cause I've been looking for her all my life."

"Now you see her. Now you don't," Jamal was sarcastic.

Then looking toward Kenali he grabs her hand from the clutches of the other man that was doing everything but drooling on her. "Come on. We need to talk."

Still holding his hand in the air as if keeping the memory of holding Kenali's hand, the other man spoke out. "Look here. You can't come disrespecting nobody like that. You don't know me."

Jamal flashed him a look with so much anger and hatred that it put fear into both of the men. The first one had to speak out.

"You betta leave young blood alone. He might be one of those crazy ones that kill up everybody."

Jamal shot a reply back to him. "It's in my blood. Like father like son."

Distance was now growing between them as he was walking almost dragging Kenali but he still was able to hear their final comments.

"Told you. There's something real wrong with young blood. I mean she fine and all but she ain't worth dying for."

Now out of eyesight and earshot of the men, Kenali planted her feet to put up some resistance from being pulled like a ragdoll by Jamal.

"You're taking me too fast. I'm not sixteen anymore and I just had a baby."

"What are you doing down here looking for me? You can get yourself hurt. Cause people crazy and you can't be knocking everywhere."

"I'm grown and not stupid. Now your mom wants you to come home. She's worried sick about you."

"She's not worried. My own mom is scared of me."

"No she's not."

"You wasn't there!" Jamal spoke from frustration.

Before replying, Kenali let out a deep breathe to slow the pace of the conversation down. "She told me. It's something in her mind that got her like that. Once you go through something like she been through you don't always bounce back completely."

"But I'm her son. I wouldn't do anything to hurt her. I didn't mean to push her. It just happened so fast. I turned and next thing I know she fell. I tried to help her up but she pulled back from me. You should have seen her eyes."

Jamal had to turn away from Kenali. He didn't want her to see the hurt that was definitely displayed in his eyes. Kenali came behind him burying the side of her face in the back of his soft curly hair. She just held him squeezing him so tight yet gently. With her hands crossed over his chest, she could feel how fast his heart was beating. Only a portion of that speed was his youthfulness. The other was pain and confusion.

"Let's go so we can fix it."

"This can't be fixed. I can't go back there. I don't belong there anymore."

"We are family."

"I don't know who I am. My whole life isn't real. It's like I'm watching TV. Too much drama."

"Your life is real. Just as real as I'm hugging you. Bad things happen to good people sometimes. If you don't want to go home, come home with me."

As Kenali slowly released him from the hug to peer around him to look into his face to search for the answer of the new deal that is on the table.

"I don't think that would be a good idea," Jamal replied half-heartedly not wanting to give up.

"It's the best idea. A whole lot better than sleeping on the streets."

"I won't have to sleep on the streets," Jamal shot back trying to convince the both of them that he had a plan.

"Shakenda can't hide you for too long."

Jamal paused. "How do you know about her?"

"Like I said, I'm not stupid."

"That much I know," Jamal replied.

"So to keep from getting her in trouble, come stay at my place. I know that your mind is racing a mile a minute but there I won't bother you so you can get your head together. So how does that sound good?"

"I don't know. You know you can't keep mama from coming over there. I need to think."

"She'll be fine as long as you're safe. I'll talk to her. But eventually you're going to have to face the situation."

"I know. Just not today. I'll get up with you later."

Kenali watched painfully as Jamal walked away from her. At least she knew where he was. He was safe for now. But his attitude was just like Divine had said; he was a ticking time bomb. She just hoped that he didn't hurt anyone or himself.

# CHAPTER 10

"Yes. His name is Christian Jackson," Lane paused listening to the response of the person on the other side of the phone. "He's not there? Thank you."

Lane hung up the phone feeling discouraged. He had called about ten facilities in the surrounding cities. There was no sign of Christian anywhere. Lane couldn't figure out what was actually going on or why Christian had just disappeared without contacting anyone.

"Any luck?" A patient Simbol walked back into the room carrying a glass of water for Lane who had been talking for what seems like all morning.

"None. I can't give up though."

"Please don't for Kenali and David's sake." Simbol was so concerned. Lane swiveled his chair to face her.

"But what's getting me upset is why Christian ain't calling." Lane leaned back in the chair with his elbow propped up on the desk. His fist covered his mouth as if to threaten the wrong words from coming out. "I mean, the only thing that I can think of is that when he woke up he was psyched out or something. He had all of his limbs; the doctors said that he would just have to learn how to walk all over again. So what's the problem?"

"I don't know baby. All I know is that Kenali is wearing herself out trying to stay hopeful, take care of David and worry about Jamal. She's good at covering up negative things but I know my sister. And she's worried." Simbol closed her eyes to compare Kenali before all of this with the new and not so improved version that she saw now.

"I still want to believe that my cuz is alright and that maybe he just needed some time to get himself together. We just don't know how the accident shook his mind up."

"That's true," she answered with understanding.

Simbol's mind went back to when she had been pushed down the stairs. Everything seemed like it was going so fast on the outside but her mind was in slow motion wondering how all of this was happening. She was never the same especially when she saw the result of the push. Shaking her head to erase the thoughts, she simply stated once again, "That is so true."

"Don't worry. I'll find him since I got a few more numbers to call. Surely he had to go to one of them."

Placing an appreciative kiss on the top of Lane's head while rubbing his shoulders, Simbol excused herself from the room. "Thanks baby. Let me know if you need me to do anything. I'll be in the kitchen."

Enjoying his new wife's touch but wishing it was under different circumstances, Lane replied, "Ok." He instantly reached for the phone to get back on the job of locating his cousin. Persistence paid off a few calls later.

"He's there?" Lane excitedly stood up as if all the energy forced him to do so. But he soon returned to his seat to jot down all the information that he was being given.

"Thank you so much. You have been so helpful." Before he could even disconnect the call he was yelling for Simbol.

"Baby, I got something."

Simbol ran out of the kitchen as if Publisher's Clearing House was at the door with a ten million dollar check.

"You found him?" She excitedly questioned.

"Yes and no. I'm on his trail."

"What do you mean?"

"He was there trying to be checked in but they didn't have any room so they directed him to another facility that was close by that did have openings. I got the information right here."

"So what are you going to do?"

"I'm going to get my cousin."

"Are you sure he's there?"

"The guy sounded pretty sure. He said that they called to see if they had room and that they were sending someone over. He stated normally when they do that, the people go there. The place is only forty-five minutes away. You want to go?"

"Grabbing my purse."

The couple was so excited as they drove. To Simbol it seemed as if they would never get there. Lane's heart was beating a mile a minute. There was something on the inside of him that was afraid to see what condition Christian was in. He prayed inwardly as they traveled with the hope that all of Kenali's and everyone else's worries were about to come to a screeching halt.

# CHAPTER 11

K enali finally got home after a long day of exhausting searches and emotional disappointment. She was glad that she at least knew where Jamal was but when he walked away from her like he did, there was more damage done to her than either one of them could imagine. In her mind, she didn't see Jamal walking away, it was Christian.

But now she was too mentally tired to focus on fighting that battle right now. David was doing his favorite thing of sleeping which was good for her at this present time. She was so thankful that he was not a fussy baby. All he wanted was to eat and sleep.

She took full advantage of it by running a hot tub of water. She felt like she could soak for an infinite amount of time. Getting undressed to slide into her private spa, she stuck her foot into the water. It was like liquid hands welcoming her to submerge to be cradled by it. Kenali really needed this bath.

She needed to release her fears, tears and tensions. Kenali had no one to vent to. Everyone else had their own issues. Surely she couldn't unload on them. So she looked to the water as she had done so many times before. Kenali had long come to the conclusion that motivators don't have people to motivate them. As always, she would release her cares upon the Lord who was faithful to hear her cry.

Then her actions were halted by the ringing doorbell. Had two guys not been absent from her life, she would have passed on answering it.

Kenali put her robe on, tying it as she went toward the door. Looking through the peep hole, she smiled to see that head of bushy curly hair that she so desperately wanted to see. She opened the door with so much force, Jamal flinched.

"You get yourself in here," Kenali jokingly stated.

"Ok but you remember our deal right?"

Kenali went over in her mind the terms of their agreement. Just about anything could pass right about now as long as he was there with her.

"Yes. I remember. I'm glad that you're here."

Jamal was going to be some work but she was up to the task. The results of that letter had done so much damage to him that he wasn't himself anymore. But she knew that time would heal all wounds.

She closed the door behind him. He quickly made himself at home since this has always been his second one. Jamal just walked straight to his room without saying a word. Kenali watched him with her heart aching to make things better for him. But she couldn't. Not right now.

She returned back to her place of solace. Kenali remembered retreating to the bathroom after her mother's funeral. Tonight she would do the very thing that she did then. She would let the water wash away her tears. As she lay with her head reclining back onto the pillow, she allowed a flood of many emotions to overcome her. Kenali grieved her mother's death. She mourned Christian's disappearance. She sorrowed over Jamal's pain.

Kenali wished so greatly that Christian would come to her just as he did after the funeral. She wished that when she had cried into the water that he would once again be standing outside of her room. This new thing to her called doubt reassured her that he wouldn't be. She cried all the more.

The sobs that were too strong, she hid them behind moments of deep inhalations. With the tears rolling from the corners of her eyes to meet up at the base of her neck, she remained motionless until she felt some sort of release. Then remembering the time, she attempted to situate herself. She didn't want to be like that around David.

No sooner than she had gotten her plush pajamas on, he began to make noises alerting her that it was feeding time. She went to him looking at how he was squirming around beneath his baby blue blanket that had the cutest satiny lamb centered on it. Pulling back the blanket, she picked him up with so much care cradling him into her arms. He settled down there knowing that mommy had heard his request.

When he was done eating, Kenali heard the TV on in the den. She knew that Jamal had come out of his room although he could have watched TV in there. Thinking to herself that she wanted to give him all the space that he needed but what if this was a sign that he wanted to talk.

Kenali decided to take David in for a visit with his big cousin hoping that he would soften Jamal's heart.

"You want some company?"

Jamal looked back over the couch where he was sitting slumped over to the side.

"Sure." He sat up straight to make room for her to sit beside him.

She eased down onto the couch. Jamal's body language didn't change much. Out of the corner of his eye he looked at David who caused Jamal to automatically smile. He listened at the conversation that Kenali was having with David. Although he wasn't a baby himself, there was something about her tone that was soothing.

"Do you want to hold him?"

Jamal was shocked that she asked him. He had never held a baby before. His little brothers didn't count since he was so young then himself.

"You sure you want me to hold him?" Jamal was acting like his dysfunction was contagious.

"I would have never offered if I didn't." Kenali wanted Jamal to know that she has never looked at him any differently than who he is.

She positioned his arm for him to receive David who was awake and looking around. His mouth was in motion as if he was still sucking.

"What's he chewing on?"

Kenali giggled at Jamal's question.

"He's not *chewing* on anything. I just fed him and he might still have some milk in his mouth that he tastes."

"Naw. He's trying to tell you he wants some more. Lil dude is greedy. Babies are easy to figure out."

"Oh really? Please tell me more." Kenali had to hear more of his logic since she hadn't found getting up to feed him every two to three hours was anywhere near easy.

"You see it's like this. He can't walk so he can't get into anything. All he's going to do is eat, sleep, and poop. Man that's the life," Jamal explained.

"One day in the distant future I'm going to remind you of this conversation and see what you and your wife have to say about it then."

Jamal just grinned looking back to David.

"So how long have you and Shakenda been an item?" Kenali easily slid the question in. After all, he was in a talking mood that was far better than earlier that day.

"For a minute," he simply replied.

"And that told me nothing."

Jamal laughed when he had to remember that he was talking to his aunt and not just one of his friends. He knew that she did make an effort to be on his level but the short terminology did her no good since she was a detailed person.

"My bad. About six months."

"You have known her for six months and not once peeped anything about it. Why not?"

"We were just talking on Facebook. You know that's a social media site that—"

"Don't be funny Jamal," Kenali laughed at his attempt to be a wise guy.

"Just checking." Jamal paused with a smile. "Then we met in person about 3months ago at the skating rink."

"Do you like her?"

"I mean yeah. She's a good person. Different from the other girls."

"Yes she is. I've known her for a minute too. Actually maybe 3 minutes cause I've known her for a year and a half. LOL."

"OMG, aunt Kenali. Please don't do that."

Kenali was glad that Jamal was coming out of his slump. Enjoying the conversation that they swapped back and forth as they sat eating dinner that was delivered, Kenali knew that Jamal was going to be alright. Jamal just needed to get his mind off of not knowing who he was and focus on who he is. He was surrounded by a family that loves him very much. One thing that she had learned about love was that it covers a multitude of faults. Even his confusion was covered and expected.

Kenali wished greatly that Christian would show back up so that Simbol or Divine wouldn't be having this conversation with David when he grew up.

Her cell began to ring.

"How is my son? I just got your text. I'm so glad that he came there. What's he doing?" Divine was rambling questions off faster than a greyhound at a dog race.

"For my sake, slow down. He's fine. He's doing his favorite thing. Eating."

Kenali looked at Jamal seeing that his countenance was changing. He was slumping back into his earlier demeanor. So she decided to end the conversation to prevent the deletion of their progress.

"But I'll call you later on. I'm really tired right now. Ok."

"I know what that means. As soon as you are alone call me, Kenali. I don't care how late it is. Bye. And thank you."

"Oh. You're welcome. We gotta take care of each other's babies. Bye."

Kenali hung up the phone waiting to see if Jamal was going to be the first to speak. He just stared into his plate.

"You know she's going to call and check up on you. She loves you Jamal. She protected you the best way that she knew how."

Jamal's brow line wrinkled. He was angry. Kenali felt that she needed to continue.

"It took me having David to understand that a mother will do anything to protect her child. I have to protect his mental as well as his physical. Even now, I try not to act like Christian being out there somewhere doesn't bother me. If I'm uneasy, David will sense it."

"Why didn't she just have an abortion? The man raped her and tried to kill her. That would have been easiest for all of us."

"That option was available to her but she just couldn't see herself doing that. She felt like she would be taking that out on you. And look at you now. You are a great young man with a lot of potential just like she knew you would be."

Jamal wasn't seeing that potential right now.

"My bloodline says that I have a fifty percent chance of being a criminal just like him."

"But God says that you have a one hundred percent chance to be who you choose to be. Turn that negative situation around into something positive. You know you are too stubborn, I mean determined to let some criminal control you."

Her words were turning over in Jamal's mind.

"I guess I just need to sleep on it."

"That's what your granddaddy says is the best way to solve any problem. You're already learning from the right side."

Kenali stood up to hug Jamal. She could feel the tension in his body. She prayed that a good night's sleep was the right recipe that he needed to make him snap back to himself.

Now she had to call Divine to put her mind at ease.

As soon as she answered, the questions started firing off.

"How's he acting? Do you think that he'll want to come home soon? Is he mad at me?"

"It's going to take time. Right now we're making progress. So you're just going to have to calm down and be patient."

"I'll calm down. But understand that you'll be acting like this one day too. It's something about your children being in situations that you don't know how to bring them out that makes you go crazy."

"I already understand. But tonight you can rest easy that your package is in safe hands."

And with that the two sisters said their goodbyes. Kenali slid into her bed so that she could get a little sleep before her son woke up needing to be fed and changed. Being a single parent wasn't easy but David was worth all the sacrifice. And so was Jamal.

.

# CHAPTER 12

"I'm here to see Christian Jackson."

Lane's heart was racing. He couldn't believe that his cousin was out of the coma to be moving around like this. When he had heard about the accident he was so worried about Kenali especially since she had just lost her mom. Now everything was going to be alright.

"He's in therapy right now. Visitors aren't allowed in there," the nurse that was sitting at the front desk gleefully explained. She seemed to be one that loved her job expressing it by being the friendliest person that Lane had ever seen in a care facility or anywhere for that fact.

"Ok. Thanks. Do you think that we can wait in his room?" Lane asked.

"Sure. He's in room 116."

As the nurse pointed in the direction of the room, Simbol could hear her heart beating in between her ears. Excitement had overtaken her just to think of what kind of joy Kenali was going to feel. Although she wanted to pick up the cell phone to tell her sister what was taking place, she had promised Lane that she wouldn't.

It all made sense. Lane wanted to see what kind of condition Christian was in since he was running like this.

Lane felt that if he was in the wrong state of mind that would be more harmful to Kenali than not knowing.

"Oh wow. Sweetie, you really found Christian," Simbol exclaimed while they were standing in the room that now housed him.

She looked around seeing the television on playing a familiar sitcom that she enjoyed herself. There was a pair of house shoes by the side of the bed which just had the covers thrown back from when he possibly got up. She saw a chair that looked very comfortable that was close to the head of the bed. Simbol envisioned Kenali sitting there talking to Christian when she came to visit.

For now she borrowed the seat as Lane crossed the room deep in thought. Watching the back of her husband, she saw a fearful concern rest upon his shoulders as he looked out the window. Inwardly, something told her to give him space to think. She thought about her dad's actions which Lane was mimicking unknowingly right now. She decided to do what she had seen her mom do so many times; quietly comfort him with her silent presence until he needed her.

"Simbol, I hope that Christian is alright," Lane spoke while still staring immovably out of the window.

"The nurse didn't seem to have much concern on her face as if something was wrong." By the time that Simbol finished the sentence she was softly by his side.

"Baby, I mean his mindset."

"Do you want me to go ask the nurse how he is mentally?"

"They don't know him enough to know if he was right or wrong. It worries me that he didn't call at least Kenali," Lane said.

"Yeah. Me too."

"You just don't know how much he loves her. I had to hear him talk about her all the time. Actually, I think that's it. He doesn't want her to see him like he is."

"Kenali, wouldn't care one way or the other. She'll be happy just to know that he's safe."

"We men think differently. If he's not able to do for himself, he's going to feel like less of a man. And he knows that if Kenali knew where he was that she would be right here seeing him in his weakness which would be damaging him more."

"You creatures are different," Simbol stated with a smile.

"Don't laugh baby. We say the same thing about you women."

"What? We are not that difficult."

"You'll never know until you fall in love with one which I don't have to worry about. But I do need you to promise that if Christian comes in here and says that he doesn't want Kenali to know where he is now that you won't say a word to her."

Simbol had to step back with a gasp.

"But she's so worried about him."

"Just trust me on this. If he needs some more time, promise that you won't say anything. I know that she's your sister but not telling her may help him out in the long run."

"How could that help him?" Simbol shot back in question.

"We think differently remember. Who knows, he might be alright once he sees us. But just in case he says don't tell her, I gotta know that you won't."

Simbol swallowed hard. Then she let out a long defeated sigh. "Ok. I won't. It's going to be hard. I just don't like seeing my little sister cry even though she tries to be so strong."

"Thank you."

"Don't thank me now. This is going to cost you."

"Oh really? What more can I give? I'm already your love slave," Lane said with a sheepish smirk arising on his face.

Simbol wrapped her arms around Lane's neck. She began to caress the base of his neck while looking him in the eyes. "Don't worry. I'll think of something great since us women think so differently."

"Alright then, Mrs. Jones." Lane gratefully lowered his head to kiss his wife and in mid stride the door flung open. He turned his head thinking that he was going to be seeing his cousin but instead he saw the nurse from the desk.

"I'm sorry but I have to tell you that I just got word that Mr. Jackson won't be coming back to his room."

"Why not?" Lane asked while releasing his wife.

"Because the ambulance had to take him to the hospital. During therapy something happened and I'm sorry that I don't have any further details but his nurse came to tell me."

"May I speak to her?"

"You can at the hospital. She went with him."

"Ok. What's her name and which hospital did they take him too?" Lane questioned.

"Her name is Kerry and he was taken to Mercy over on the south side of town. Are you familiar with its location?"

"Yes. Thanks."

As the chipper little nurse spun to go back out of the room another question popped into Lane's head stopping the nurse before she could even get out of the room.

"Why didn't they just treat him here?" Lane asked.

"There are certain levels of treatment that we can administer here. If it's something like surgery then the patient has to be taken to the hospital. Due to him being in a coma for so long it causes the bones to weaken and the potential for him to break one is great especially if he puts too much pressure on it or even move wrong. So don't worry. We are going to take the best care of him," the friendly nurse confirmed.

"Alright. Thanks again."

"You're welcome," the nurse scaled the pitch of her voice to almost sing the words. It seems as if she was excited to be of service.

"Now I see why you don't want me to tell Kenali. She would've gotten excited for nothing. Talk about an emotional rollercoaster."

"I know right. Let's go to the hospital."

As they rode over to the hospital, Lane's premonition that something else was going on with Christian rose back up. What if this was God's way of letting him know that now isn't the time for him to see Christian? Even worse, what if Christian had made up his mind that loving Kenali was too much of a sacrifice? Regardless of where his mind was, Lane was even more determined to see Christian so that he can let him know that he has a wonderful son that he needs to raise.

# CHAPTER 13

K enali woke up with the sun shining in her face. Mentally examining herself, she realized that she had slept very hard yet peacefully. She looked over to David's crib. When she saw him still asleep she knew that he didn't have any requests other than for the sleep itself. His lips were in the sucking motion as if they still contained the memory of the pacifier that was beside him. He and she both had every right to be tired after the eventful day they had yesterday.

Thinking about yesterday reminded her that Jamal was in the house. Under the current circumstances, acting afraid of him would have not been the solution to his healing process. Out of all the people that she had motivated, he was going to be the toughest considering his age and him being a family member.

This barrier is Kenali's new task that would have to be placed on the back burner for now. She had two young men to feed two very different meals. Since there was a deep growling in her stomach she knew that Jamal's would be like a volcano erupting. It was late when they ate and somehow it felt as if she hadn't eaten in years.

When she opened the door to her bedroom, she whiffed the scents of food in the air. Amazingly, nothing smelled burnt.

"Wow. When did you learn how to cook?"

Kenali's eyes were looking at a feast that was laid before her. Jamal had cooked pancakes, bacon, eggs and hash browns. Everything looked so good that she wouldn't have thought that a teenage boy made this meal.

"Dad taught me some years ago." Then Jamal thought about what he said then decided to make amendments. "Or at least Mr. Gerald did."

"Jamal, Gerald is still your dad. The title is based on the action. He raised you. Worked to make sure you had a good life with a roof over your head and all the necessities plus a lot of extras. I can't think of one time that he treated you any different from your brothers. That man loves you as his own. In his eyes, you are his son."

Jamal dropped his head as if her spoken words weighed so heavily within his mind. Then Kenali knew that she had to break the thickness that was in the air.

"Are you sure you don't have Paula Deen or the Neelys in here somewhere? This spread looks so good that if David sees it, he's going to wish that he had teeth."

It worked. Now Jamal was blushing in a cocky way. She was going to have to deal with him very gently. He is fragile. Time is what he needed. She couldn't even begin to imagine what he was dealing with on the inside. Outside of the issues that he was facing, he was a male. Gerald would be the person to deal with it but Jamal had shut everyone out but her. She refused to let him down.

Then Kenali's mind went to a place called *if Christian were here*. If Christian were here she thought, he would be the perfect help. He grew up without knowledge of who his father was until the man was about to die. The circumstances were different but they both involved absenteeism.

"So what do you want to do today?" Jamal asked breaking into her thoughts.

"I don't know. What do you want to do?"

"You answered a question with a question."

"That's right. Let me give you a tip. You don't talk to a hungry woman about future plans that don't involve getting married while she's eating a great meal that she didn't have to cook. That's just rude," Kenali joked.

Jamal's only alternative was to join her in laughter while she still forked food into her mouth.

"If you can't beat 'em then join 'em. Let me get a plate before you clean house."

"You sound like a very wise young man."

"I had to wise up. You eating faster than me."

"I'm glad that you cooked. I was so hungry that my stomach was growling in HD."

"Oh that's what I heard. I thought the garbage truck kept passing by the house."

"No you didn't go there. But that was a good one," Kenali giggled almost choking.

The two continued to swap jokes and conversation over this meal that was so gratefully appreciated. Jamal wanted to show his aunt gratitude for allowing him to stay there while Kenali was grateful to have some company to take her mind off Christian.

Although she wanted to know where he was, she just didn't have the strength to search for him. With all the late night feedings, getting up and down every couple of hours, she chose to use that energy to lovingly give her son what he couldn't provide for himself.

Deep down on the inside, the day that she went to unsuccessfully see Christian, it damaged her in ways that she didn't even understand. Now she had to focus on the two young men that were underneath her roof at this time. Besides, as far as the heart is concerned, they were safer.

# CHAPTER 14

"How could he not be here? We were told he was brought here," Lane stated in a very irritated tone.

"Sir, we haven't received anybody by that name or from that facility."

Lane was totally irritated now along with confused about what was going on. He couldn't figure out how Christian couldn't be here when he was told that he was sent here. His gut feeling was that something was going on and he was going to get to the bottom of it.

Simbol was just as confused as he was. Had Lane come back home to tell her that he was involved in all of these events she probably would have thought that he was exaggerating. She was an eyewitness to this instead, growing more to understand that her husband was right in not telling Kenali. She had too much going on already to be involved into this rollercoaster of a ride.

"Do you have another location since the nurse specified this one?" Simbol and Lane were tag teaming the receptionist with questions.

"Yes, we do. Let me call over there to see if perhaps he was sent there."

While she was on the phone, the couple swapped looks and then back to her for any indication on her face that she was coming up with an appropriate answer. Then she thanked the person on the other line before hanging up.

"I'm sorry but they don't have him either. I don't know what else to tell you but to go back to where you came from. Maybe they made a mistake in what they told you."

"Alright. Thanks," Lane spoke very dryly although it had nothing to do with her. His frustration was building so fast the double sliding doors almost didn't have enough time to open. Simbol was walking, actually running to keep up with his pace. She had never seen him like this yet she knew he had good reason.

"Lane, what's going on?"

"I don't know but I'm about to find out."

When hc pulled back into the parking lot of the rehabilitation center, he attempted to calm himself. He didn't like to be toyed with. He felt the old Lane rising up. He wanted to handle this situation like he would if he was still running the streets. So he lowly made a quick prayer for help.

"Lord, please help me. Please."

Simbol looked at the side of his face knowing what he was saying although she could barely hear him. His value skyrocketed in her eyes right then for she knew that she had a praying man. And his prayers became effective as a slightly familiar voice cried out to them from one of the parked cars.

"How's your cousin?"

They turned to see the helpful nurse that told them that Christian had been transported to the hospital. She was getting ready to leave but as they walked towards her car she put it in park and opened the door to get out talking with them.

"He wasn't there. So they sent us back here," Simbol explained.

"What?" she questioned before speaking her new thoughts. "There are two locations. Maybe he's at the other one. I'll call to see if he's there."

Now Lane interjected. "They called. He's not there either."

The lady who was short in stature with a petite frame now looked at them over the top of her square shaped glasses in disbelief. The smile was wiped clean off her face to become replaced by determination.

"Follow me. And by the way my name is Fran."

They followed Fran as her short legs took her swiftly back into the rehab. Then she walked up to the desk as if she was a visitor. Fran let them know who Lane and Simbol were and that she was helping them. Next she went to Christian's room to see it cleaned out. There were no signs that Christian had been there other than the bed that showed that someone slept there.

"I don't like this. Please have a seat," Fran dramatically stated.

Lane and Simbol obeyed her command as she stood looking as if she was a doctor coming in to explain the procedure that was about to be done on a loved one.

"I don't know what's going on but I don't like it. I was a little suspicious of his nurse the first day that they got here."

"His nurse? She came with him." Simbol was sharp since she was analyzing her every word.

"Yes. Here at the facility we just provide rehabilitation services. The individual or family has to provide the in room care if it's needed. Most people hire a private sitter or have a family member take care of them. That's not unusual. But what was unusual is that I never heard anything about his family. I tried to ask him and she would always interrupt. Then one day I heard him tell her that he wished that he could remember."

"So Christian has amnesia?" Simbol almost screeched.

Christian with amnesia was a whole lot better to deal with than one that was just running for no apparent reason.

"That's my opinion based on how he acted and what I overheard," Fran commented.

"So do you have any contact information for the nurse?" Lane wanted to know who she was and why she was moving his cousin around like this.

"Yes. A cell phone. But it's no good."

"How do you know?" Simbol blurted out.

"When you left to go to the hospital, I called it to check on Mr. Jackson. It was disconnected. We don't have any other information for her. The only thing that I know is that she identified herself as Nurse Kerry and that was it."

"We really appreciate your help. Can you think of anything else?" Lane was sitting on the edge of his seat.

"Yes!" She jolted to speak. "There is one other thing. She's pregnant."

Lane and Simbol had to look at one another for support. This tale was getting crazier by the moment.

"How many months?" Simbol asked.

"I don't know because she never talked to us much but to judge it, I would say about seven months. She looks as if she is close to her due date."

"One more thing. Since he has amnesia, how did she act toward him?" Lane leaned to the side as if he was an interrogator trying to see the truth from every angle.

"She acted like they were more than nurse and patient. But I could tell that it was more like that she wanted it to be more."

Fran was so happy to be of service. Just working at the front desk was stifling her growth but for this she was able to put on her detective hat which brought some drama to her possibly boring life.

Lane and Simbol walked out of the rehab without knowing where Christian was but they were armed with more information than they knew before. Now they just had to find a way to keep this information from Kenali until they actually found Christian. She could deal with the amnesia but having to handle another delusional woman that is trying to dig her clutches into her man might prove that the city was far too small for that fight.

Sitting behind the steering wheel just clutching it, Lane finally spoke what was in his mind.

"When we find Christian, which we will, remind me to ask him how he keeps attracting these crazy women?"

# CHAPTER 15

"It's hard to imagine you with a baby, aunt Kenali," Jamal said while shaking his head in disbelief.

Kenali smiled as she thought about how hard it was for her to imagine it also. She continued to change David's diaper still thinking of how wonderful it was. He was such a good baby who hardly ever had fussy moments or crying spells. It was going to be pretty much quiet or cooing. She wasn't upset at all about it either.

"Why is it so hard to imagine?"

"Cause you are, you know, old."

"What?!"

"I mean you're not exactly young." Jamal trying to get himself out of the doghouse wasn't working. He was only digging deeper with every passing word.

"Now could be a good time to zip it. The more you open your mouth the worse it gets," Kenali reassured him.

Making the motion that he was zipping his lips and throwing away the key, Jamal knew that Kenali wasn't offended by his words. Then he pretended to be retrieving the key to unlock his mouth.

"But you're so cool though. David got a real good mom."

"I know right." Kenali was blushing from her eyes as well. She had already been thinking of how to be the best possible mommy to David. "And you have a good mom too, Jamal."

"I know," Jamal didn't even hesitate to answer. He was definitely thinking on it.

Since he was in agreement, Kenali decided to just walk through this opened door.

"Will you help me to understand how you feel on the inside since the day you found out?"

Jamal took a moment to search for his words.

"I'm so confused. It's like I know who I am but then I don't. I feel like I am living a lie. I don't know how I'm supposed to act now."

"Did you start feeling like this when you read the letter?"

"Yes and no. Most of it did. I already had some questions but everybody kept telling me that I was changing cause I was getting older."

Jamal just stopped talking. Kenali paused before saying anything since he was getting it out. She didn't want to stop the flow of his progress. Then just as she suspected he started to speak again.

"I don't want to be like him. He hurt my mom. I keep trying to consider her feelings but this thing is riding me. I got his DNA. Honestly, isn't there a chance that I could be like him?" Jamal was looking sincerely at Kenali almost praying that the answer would be 'no'.

"No sweetheart. You have control over who you will become. Plus you're surrounded by too many prayer warriors to become like him. I'm sorry that your mom had to go through what she did but I'm glad that you're here. You're an amazing person and I want you to hang around David so that he can be like you. I always said that I want a son like you and that hasn't changed now."

Just knowing that made Jamal's heart rejoice. He began to feel much better about himself than he had in the previous days. Although he still didn't feel good enough to go home to face that music he was just going to bask in better for now. That word was becoming a giant within his mind. He began to feel like he would be better than the evil within his real father.

Even when the text came in from Shakenda asking how he was doing, he simply replied, 'better'. It was good that she text him. She was going to be the next person that he contacted after he and Kenali finished talking. It felt good to Jamal to be thought about.

"Thanks auntie. I feel better."

"You're welcome. Anytime you need to talk, I'm here."

"You know, David got himself a really good mom." As he was walking away he decided to interject one more sly comment. "Your mind works pretty good for an old chic."

Kenali gasped. Before she knew it, she had flung some of David's socks at him. Jamal playfully fell in slow motion as if he had been knocked down.

"Now take that. I'm not old. I'm in my thirties. You better recognize, Boo."

There was never a dull moment around Jamal. She enjoyed the time that he was with her. She knew that he was going to be alright after some time and a few more Q&A sessions. Soon she was going to have to face her own reality by answering some questions of her own dealing with where's the father of her baby.

# CHAPTER 16

Opening her eyes more and more to reality, Simbol sent her arm to investigate the other side of the bed only to realize that it felt as it did before she was married. The sheets were cool to the touch, still crisp on that side.

Lane had not even come to bed at all were her thoughts. Then she pried her face from the pillow which so enticingly held her while throwing the cover back so that her body could be released to search for her husband.

Sliding her feet into her slippers she walked into the bathroom for two reasons. The first became a negative when her hubby wasn't there. Then she settled for the other. Now she slipped into her robe which was hanging on the back of the door. Momentarily, she got jealous because the door was draped by this satiny coolness that now covered every bare part of her body with stunningly cool satisfaction. Even better was the fact that her husband had bought it for her bridal shower. Somehow he was able to sneak it onto the mound of gifts unnoticed.

Opening the door to the bedroom, Lane was still nowhere in sight. Calling out his name yielded no results either.

Simbol continued to walk around the house until she spotted him through the window.

Lane was still fully dressed sitting under the tree in the backyard. She wondered if he had slept out there since those lawn chairs were super comfortable. By the time that she reached him, she knew that he hadn't slept much at all. The tension on his face worried her enough that she covered him with her arms.

"Sorry I didn't come to bed last night," Lane automatically said as soon as Simbol touched him.

"It's ok. Did you get any sleep?"

"I fell asleep at the computer. I didn't want to wake you so I laid on the couch."

"How long have you been out here?"

"About an hour or so."

"I know you're worried about Christian but you still have to get your rest," Simbol spoke with volumes of concern in her voice.

"Baby, my mind just wouldn't shut down. I want to know so many things about this nurse chic. Who hired her? Who got her pregnant? And why is she doing this?"

Not being able to answer any of those questions, Simbol continued silently cleaving to her husband. Then Lane continued.

"It's almost like Julia is taunting us from the grave."

Just the thought of that woman sent chills over Simbol's body. Julia caused their family so much stress in their time of grief. All the things that she did to Christian and Kenali were on such a psychotic level of desperation that the only counterattack they could come up with outside of hiring a hit man was prayer.

Now it seems as if they were going to have to band together again to accomplish Christian's reemergence into their lives for the sake of them all.

"It might seem like that but just know that we're going to put an end to this...again," Simbol spoke so confidently that Lane almost wanted to check to see if she was still the one holding him.

It was refreshing to have a spiritually positive woman on his side. And she was right. This had been going on long enough. It was time for Kenali and Christian to be together happily ever after like they both wanted to be before all this took place.

That thought alone, spurred new questions in the mind of Lane.

"Do you think that he'll remember us? I don't think that he will since he hadn't called," Lane was answering his own questions. Simbol was thinking as he rambled on.

"I did some research last night on amnesia and there are different versions of it. Some of it only lasts for a short time but others can be permanent. Just like trauma put him in it sometimes trauma can reverse it. If we can get to him then we can start jarring his memory," Lane stated almost sounding like all the pages of expert writings that he had read.

"How do you plan on doing that? Fake a car accident or something?" Simbol wondered.

"No. I got some photos from our childhood plus some recent ones. I can show them to him when we find him. If he doesn't remember right off the bat then at least he'll know that we know him."

Lane felt that he would succeed. If only he could get to Christian. He was worried that the longer that he was away the harder it would be for him to get his memory back. From

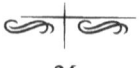

the way that Simbol's body stiffened sending her to stand straight up; something had jolted a memory in her.

"Let's go to the hospital." She looked as if she was entranced by something off in the distance.

"Back to the hospital we were at last night?" Lane questioned.

Breaking her trance, looking at Lane now, a sneaky little smile replaced the widened eyes that she once displayed.

"No. To the hospital that he was at for almost a year. Maybe that's where this Nurse Kerry came from."

"Great idea. Let's go."

Simbol hurried to get dressed as if she were in some sort of speed dressing competition. She was so inspired by finding the truth that she forfeited some of her usual routines. They weren't as important as finding out who this woman was and why she was doing this.

When they pulled up to the hospital, she barely could wait for Lane to put the truck in park. She didn't even wait for him to open the door for her to get out. As soon as he got to her side she was already in mid stride heading for the elevator. Her ponytail was bouncing with her every step. The only thing that allowed Lane to catch up was she had to wait for the elevator. He knew that if the stairs would have been nearby she would have sprinted up them.

"Slow down, baby. We don't want to seem like we want to know about this nurse because she was our supplier."

Simbol snickered. "I just got excited." As soon as she said it, the bell dinged, the doors opened and she was off again. By the time the elevator opened, it was like releasing a speed skater. She got to the exit of the parking garage, crossed the street, entered the hospital and was on the floor that had been home to Christian for so long.

It was perfect that she had been down there enough times with Kenali and Divine that the nurses still remembered her. After getting into a friendly little chat about the baby, Kenali and everybody else, Simbol soon worked their hearts over.

"Everything is ok but there's one thing that would make everything better. Lil David doesn't have a daddy and we found out that Christian has amnesia. We're on his trail but we need your help to bring David's daddy home to him."

The nurses were gathered around at full attention as they were the day that Kenali brought David to the hospital.

"I really thought that those two were probably married by now. We'll help you in any way that we can," one of the nurses exclaimed.

"Good. There's a name that keeps popping up. She's actually with Christian but we don't know why. The name is Kerry. She's a nurse," Simbol paused to scan the reactions of their faces.

"What?" One of the nurses vocally displayed her surprise. "She was the nurse that mainly took care of Christian for the last couple of months while he was here."

"Does she still work here?"

"She went on a leave of absence about a month ago."

"Because she was in the last stages of her pregnancy?" Simbol questioned.

"Pregnancy? She wasn't pregnant as far as I could tell. And she definitely wasn't in her last stages."

This was getting weirder by the minute. So weird that Lane and Simbol looked at each other in total disbelief.

"So she wasn't pregnant and she's not here anymore? We just thought that maybe it was the same person," Simbol sounded puzzled.

"Have you seen her?" One of the nurses asked.

"No. The lady at the rehab said that was her name and that she was very pregnant. Is there any kind of way that we can see her picture or get a copy?" Simbol asked almost pleading.

One of the nurses came forward immediately crushing Lane and Simbol's bubbles. "No we can't. We don't have access to any of that stuff. I'm sorry that we can't help you. I'll walk you out and answer any other questions that you might have. Besides I was the one that was here the most plus I'm on break."

As the other ladies went back to work feeling the need to help more but none of them wanted to lose their jobs by giving out personal info. So as the three of them got farther away, the more they returned back to their job duties erasing any spy tactics out of their brains.

Once in the elevator, the nurse started talking again.

"I didn't want to talk in front of them. I can get you the info that you need but you didn't get it from me if you know what I mean. I have a family to feed."

"We understand," Simbol relayed to her with the security that it would go no further than the three of them.

"Your sister is a great person who did more than sit here with her fiancé every day. She helped my whole family out. That's why I thought that it was strange when I got reassigned from being Mr. Jackson's nurse. Kenali was on bed rest and '*they*' said that she requested a different nurse. Next thing you know I was out and Kerry was in. I always knew that Kenali didn't ask for those changes but she wasn't here. So I couldn't prove it."

The elevator came to a halt and the nurse got quiet once again. Lane and Simbol followed in understanding, while she led them outside of the hospital to a very noisy spot by several huge air conditioning units. Then she began to talk again as they huddled around to hear.

"I'll get the info for you. Meet me at the riverfront at 7pm. If I'm a little behind, it's because I got held over but I will be there. I'll tell you everything then."

"Ok. Thank you so much. We'll see you then," Simbol said.

Then the nurse just walked off without saying anything else. As they went in the opposite direction, Lane and Simbol couldn't believe how this was unfolding. It felt eerie as well as unreal. Not knowing what else that she was going to tell them kept them on pins and needles all day long.

Simbol tried to act normal as she talked to Kenali on the phone. She hated to turn Kenali's invite down but she had to. It was too close to the time that they were to meet with the nurse that held the key to all the questions of what was going on.

If she could explain that to Kenali it would have been better but she just chose to make marital excuses.

"I'm sorry sis, but Lane and I have made plans for the night. I promise you that I'll make it up to you tomorrow."

And of course Kenali understood. They were newlyweds. One day when she found out the real truth, she would thank them for sparing her from the intrigue. This tale was untwisting in a way that even Lane and Simbol thought that there was no way possible that it could be reality. But they knew better. In just a few short intense hours they would have another piece to the puzzle.

# CHAPTER 17

"So have you come up with any suggestions as to what we can do today?" Kenali asked.

"We could go to the amusement park," Jamal excitedly replied.

"I have a baby that's not ready for that yet."

"Oh yeah. I don't know what I was thinking. Ummm? We could go get some movies to watch. Then crash around eating pizza and drinking pop."

"You just got finished eating and you're still thinking about food?" Kenali was amazed at how Jamal could eat so much and still remain pencil thin. The only thing that she could guess was that the food was either going to his hair or to his feet.

"That's my life. I live to eat," Jamal proudly stated with a look of satisfaction on his face.

Kenali let go of the food topic to venture elsewhere.

"What do you think Shakenda is up to?" Kenali treaded carefully.

"Can she come over?" Jamal rushed to ask.

"Now look who's answering a question with a question. Sure she can come if it's alright with her mom. You can go pick her and the movies up."

"For real?"

"If her mom says it's ok. Actually, I may have to pick her up cause I need to talk to her mom."

"I knew that you weren't going to let me drive," Jamal said coming back down from his quick excitement.

"You've driven my car before. Have you lost your license since then or something?"

"Nope I still got them. Her mom probably wouldn't let her go with me anyways. She acts like she doesn't like me."

"Aw. He doesn't know how to take it when someone doesn't like him."

"I'm straight." Jamal now tried to straighten his clothes up as if he was alright. Kenali knew that he did that when he didn't understand something. Like the back of her hand she had this young man's actions down to a 'T'.

"Sure you are. Well call her to see if she wants to come over. I'm going to get David dressed."

Kenali walked off to go to her bedroom. Jamal dug his cell phone out of his pocket in cool excitement. It felt good to be around people that didn't care who he was or who his real father was.

While he keyed in her number, he couldn't remember why he hadn't told his family about her anyway. Then he remembered why. It meant telling them that he was sneaking across town. Now he wasn't worried about telling his mom how they met. He knew that his aunt Kenali would smooth that over for him. Those sisters just knew how to handle one another.

"Hey whatcha doing?" Jamal put on the most suave voice that he owned to mask the boyish joy that he really felt.

"Nothing. Just hanging at the house," Shakenda replied.

"Do you want to come over to my auntie's house to hang out with us?"

"What? How will I get there?" Shakenda responded in shock. She was not expecting to be asked that question.

"She's gonna scoop you up. She said something about needing to talk to your mom anyway."

"My mom? What about?" Shakenda was a little worried. She could only hope that Kenali wasn't going to tell her where she found Jamal. Her mother wasn't the understanding type especially when it came to a certain person.

"Don't know," Jamal simply replied.

"Do you think she'll tell my mom that you were here?"

"No. Aunt Kenali is cool peeps. She would get you out of trouble before she got you into it."

Shakenda felt some relief. Even though she knew Kenali from the center she still wasn't sure of her total personality.

Jamal still waited for a response to his earlier question and decided to remind Shakenda of it. "So do you wanna come?"

"Yeah that would be cool but I have to ask my mom. I already know what she's going to say. So let me call you back."

Shakenda already knew that she was going to have to hear about how people like Jamal was only going to use her. That they don't marry girls from where they live and blah, blah, blah, blah. She couldn't figure out how to get through to her mother about Jamal being different from other boys and even greater about how different she felt from everyone around there. Shakenda always had the feeling that she wasn't going to let her geography dictate her altitude in life. She was determined to come up out of there. She was going to make it. She had to.

"Yeah you keep saying that but what happens when you get pregnant and he runs off. How can you make it then with a baby on one hip and bills on the other? I'm trying to tell you for your own good to stay away from them."

"But mama, Jamal isn't like that. He doesn't try anything. He shows more respect for me than those knuckleheads that I have to pass by everyday going to the bus stop."

"Whatever. Just give him time and he'll show you how much he respects you. That lady don't care nothing about you either. People with a little money and status are sick. She probably wants to use you to satisfy him anyway."

With her mama's back being turned to her, Shakenda rolled her eyes. That was a gesture that she better not let her mama see. "Why are you so bitter towards everybody? Besides she has something that she wants to talk to you about."

When Shakenda said that, her mother almost dropped the dish that she was washing in the sink when she spun around so fast. With suds dripping from her hands, she popped her neck.

"What do she need to talk to me about?" Her words were fierce with a snap.

"Ma, I don't know what she wants. I was just relaying the message," Shakenda sounded defeated in her words but her actions showed otherwise. Inside, Shakenda felt like her mom was going to let her go after Ms. Kenali talked to her. Before getting dressed she just simply sent Jamal a text that said, *"Get n dressed."*

After her response, Jamal replied, *"ok"*. Now he had to go put on some fresh gear of his own.

In the meanwhile, Kenali was in her room dressing David, looking at him while thinking about Jamal and

Shakenda. She couldn't resist the urge to think about in sixteen years from now would her son have those same problems getting together with a young lady. It just seemed that now it was so troublesome for people that wanted to be together.

A single teardrop fell from her eyes to land on David who was completely unaware. He was so fixated at how her hair cascaded to hover above him.

"Mommy is going to find your daddy. I promise. And please don't be mad at mommy if she just acts like she doesn't want to. I'm afraid to know the answer of why he's running. What if I can't handle the truth?"

Kenali took a deep sigh while wiping the tears from her eyes. It just felt good to say these things out loud so that she could find a temporary release. She knew that they didn't affect David one way or the other.

What kept swarming through her mind was not only if she could handle the truth but more so what was the truth? She did know her immediate truth. Having Jamal around did help her to take her focus off of some of the worry. Now she was going to be in the company of two teens with all their self-induced dramatic states that gave them something to do. Once they hit adulthood they will realize that they don't have to create it or wish for it since it just sort of follows you around. She was the prime example that drama just loves some people.

The knock at her door disturbed her thoughts.

"Come in."

"Auntie, I'm dressed. Don't I look fie?"

"Well you look nice. I don't know about the fie thingy that you're talking about."

Jamal just stood there in stillness blinking thinking of a way to explain the terminology. She worked with teens. How could she not know what that meant?

"Fie means…um—"

"Jamal, I know what fie means. I was just messing with you," Kenali laughed.

"Cool. Cause I was thinking that you're getting old for real."

"Tread carefully. My hand is always loaded with something and this time it's not socks but a dirty diaper."

"Ewww. I won't call you old no more. I promise."

"Smart child."

"Shakenda said that she was getting dressed."

"Alright. Let me pack his bag and we'll be heading out."

As they arrived at Shakenda's place, they saw her mom outside sweeping the small porch. Kenali could tell that this woman wasn't sweeping to clean the floor but whatever was on her mind. She was sweeping so hard but nothing was there as far as Kenali could tell.

Kenali had only met her once. Even then she seemed to be extremely stern. But Kenali knew that was because she wanted the best for her daughter. Even though Jamal couldn't understand why she didn't like him, Kenali was starting to the more she watched her sweep.

She was so absorbed in her task that Kenali decided to speak while she was still at a distance. The last thing that she wanted was to be whacked by a broom especially since she was holding David.

"Hello Mrs. Mead."

She stopped sweeping as if she was upset that someone was disturbing her. Not even looking up from the concrete that had her stilly mesmerized, she decided to correct Kenali.

"*Ms.* Mead. I never married," she boldly spoke with emphasis on Ms.

"Oh. I'm sorry."

Now two eyes were piercingly looking toward Kenali and Jamal with a reply that was equally as cold.

"You're sorry that I never married?"

"No. That I called you by the wrong title."

Kenali wished that she could say what was really in her head. *'Yes, I'm sorry that you didn't get married because if you would have maybe you wouldn't be so hateful acting like you need a man.'* If she said it, she knew that it would be followed by gunshots.

Ignoring Kenali's apology, Ms. Mead coldly switched the subject.

"My daughter said that you wanted to talk to me," her tongue was sharp. Ms. Mead was now standing with one hand on her hip while the other supported the broom.

"Yes I do have—," Kenali began.

"About what?"

Kenali was still stuck in the middle of the sentence. Now this level of rudeness she couldn't understand. She wouldn't blame Jamal if he wanted to go get back in the car. Kenali wanted to also. It wasn't out of fear of Ms. Mead but out of the fear of what Kenali really wanted to say to her.

"Well, I was wondering if Shakenda could intern during the school breaks."

"Doing what?"

"With her writing."

"Will she get paid? Cause don't nobody work for free. People try to give things a fancy name but all they mean is free labor." Ms. Mead was so sharp in her negative tone.

"No, that's not it at all. She will be getting paid while learning and fine tuning her skill," Kenali reassured.

"And what skill is that?" Ms. Mead turned her evil eye to Jamal as if she was accusing him of something before he actually did it.

Kenali was wondering if Ms. Mead was listening to anything other than the roaring, crackling fire that was burning between her ears. This lady's mindset was stuck in hell and torment.

"The skill of writing. Your daughter is an excellent writer and if—,"

Once again, this woman cut Kenali off in the middle of her sentence.

"If she so excellent then why does she need to intern?"

"Because she's excellent for her age but still needs some training to go along with that to help her for the next stage."

"Why do you care so much about her stages of life?"

"I want to see her prosper in life."

"So you want her to be a charity case? We don't take handouts around here. I believe that if you work hard enough then you will prosper and I don't need anybody trying to make themselves feel better by putting me on the list to get a handout." Ms. Mead was enflamed without a cause.

Kenali knew exactly what to do for this woman now. She was bitter beyond measure and Kenali was going to have to kill that part of her to keep Ms. Mead from killing her daughter's dreams.

"I've had to work hard for whatever I wanted. That's how I was raised. Do honest work, save up for what you want and get it the right way so that you can sleep at night without having to keep one eye open. I sleep good every night." Kenali cleared her throat before continuing. "My agenda is to teach other young people the same thing so that they don't become a statistic. And before you cut me off, I'm not saying that Shakenda will become a statistic. She's an amazing young lady that will go far in life and make you proud if you let her. I'm just trying to show her the way so that it won't be so hard and she can get there and be better than me at a younger age."

"Why would you want her to be better than you?" Ms. Mead was still snapping bitterly.

"When I pushed my son out, it wasn't easy. But carrying him for all this time made me different in ways that I never knew that it would. I want him to be better than me. Don't you want that for your daughter?"

Kenali had now slightly gotten on common ground with Ms. Mead. She hadn't won the war but this round was fine.

"Of course I do. I'll think about it."

"Thank you Ms. Mead. And one other thing."

Kenali wasn't sure if she should ask or not since just talking about something that would happen during the school breaks was such a daunting task.

Ms. Mead put her stern face back on again. "And what's that?"

"I was wondering if Shakenda could spend some time with me, my baby, and Jamal today?"

"Is this part of your internship? I thought that you said that it was during school breaks?"

"No. It's not a part of that. It's just me needing to be around some positive people today and have some good laughs to take my mind off some things that's going on in my life."

"And who's going to keep an eye on those two?"

"I am."

"You don't seem to be a good one to keep an eye on anybody. You got a baby but no wedding band. So like I said who's going to keep an eye on them?"

Ouch. Kenali felt like she had been kicked in the ribs. This lady had some nerve and now she was going to find out what nerve Kenali had.

"Like I said, I want better for these young people than I had just like you do, *Ms.* Mead."

With the emphasis that Kenali placed on the title, Ms. Mead was either going to chase her out of the yard with that broom or remember what mistakes that she made in life and calm down.

Ms. Mead thought for a moment. "She needs to be back by 8."

"We'll see you then."

Kenali could not believe she had won against this woman. Even though she knew that it was some stuff in her that still was going to make every visit a trial and tribulation, at least it was behind her this day.

As the four of them set off to enjoy the rest of the day, Kenali was still focusing on Ms. Mead's last blow. She had to shake her bitter tongued comments from her mind. Kenali knew all too well her own situation and if Ms. Mead really knew the entire story then she would not have given her such a hard time. But then again, she probably wouldn't have been any different.

For now, Kenali was dismissing that hypocritical comment before it ruined her dream of finding Christian and being the family that she knew that they were meant to be. Kenali didn't want to have the *Ms. never married* conversation with anyone ever.

# CHAPTER 18

"It's 7:30. I don't know why we didn't get her cell number." Simbol tapped impatiently on the window seal of Lane's truck.

"Baby, she probably got held over. There could've been an emergency. That is what she said."

"I know, Lane. I'm just excited to get to the bottom of this."

Lane got out of the truck and went around to the passenger's side to open the door for his anxious wife. Grabbing her hand with a smile, he began to reminisce.

"Do you remember when we doubled with Christian and Kenali and came down here after dinner? Our first date."

Now a blushing Simbol held Lane's hand as he led her to the exact spot that they sat. This was the peaceful place that they held their first of many conversations. She remembered every word that he said to her as if it was just a few minutes ago.

"When we sat right here and talked, I made up in my mind that you were going to be my wife. I had liked you even when I was running the streets. It was Christian that pushed the issue that got us together."

"Yeah. I remember his push very well but I'm over it since it worked. I really wished that he could have been at the wedding."

"Me too," Lane replied sadly.

By this time, Lane saw someone approaching them out of the corner of his eye. Then he turned all the way to see that it was the nurse.

"I'm sorry I'm late but I got held up."

"No you're fine. Have a seat." Lane stood up yielding his seat on the bench beside Simbol to this middle aged woman that he figured had been on her feet all day.

"Thank you. These shoes aren't as comfortable as they look. But to cut to the chase, my name is Margaret."

Simbol took her focus off Margaret's shoes to respond. "It's nice to meet you. I'm Simbol and this is my husband Lane. And thank you so much for what you're doing."

"You're welcome. Don't forget that you didn't get any of this information from me," Margaret reiterated with a very cautious look in her eye.

"What are you talking about? I just found this information on the internet." Lane played the clueless role precisely.

"That's what I'm talking about. You're my kind of guy." Margaret smiled before presenting what she had gotten. "First, I got you a picture of Kerry, her resume, address and phone number. All the information that we had in the system. Now to give you what isn't there."

Lane and Simbol both tuned in with extra focus. They didn't want to miss anything.

"She came to work at the hospital shortly after your cousin got there. I don't know how she got in because the hiring was on a freeze. The rumor is that she slept her way in if you know what I mean."

Margaret looked up to Lane and back to Simbol who were both very attentive to her every word.

"She had moved here from New York," Margaret continued.

"That's where Christian had the accident," Lane interjected to show that he was paying attention as well as piecing some stuff together.

"Exactly. She worked at the hospital that he was at. And check this out. She was his nurse there the majority of the time."

"So it's possible that he knew her since he lived there for a few years. Do you think she came to Alabama because Kenali had Christian transferred back to here?" Simbol had her own theories and questions as well. Then she stopped talking to look back at Margaret waiting for what she had to say next.

"She had been working at the hospital in a different department until guess when?"

"When Kenali went on bed rest," Lane responded very quickly.

"Yes sir. That's right. The reason that I remember it so well is because they gave the reason that they were moving her in to care for him was because Kenali had requested a different nurse to care for Christian. What they didn't know is that before Kenali left she told me to take care of him. And I just thought that Nurse Kerry wanted to move up or something. I didn't start piecing everything together until that day Kenali came by the hospital with the baby and didn't know that Christian was gone."

"Wow. That was a hard day for her." Simbol remembered the sound of Kenali's voice as she attempted to plaster strength and positivity over her disappointment.

"I thought the poor child was going to pass out cause she thought that we were saying that he was dead. So after that I got to digging. I didn't know what to do with the information that I had cause I didn't want to lose my job but right is right and my God will provide. So when you two popped in there today, I knew of a way that I could help her back."

Out of curiosity, Lane had to ask why she had to help her back. He noticed that she said that earlier that day as well. "Why do you keep saying she helped you? If you don't mind me asking, what did she do for you?"

"No. I don't mind not one bit. Kenali was kind of counseling my teenage grandson after school there at the hospital some days. She helped him get on track and he has been doing good ever since. Then she gave me some advice to give to my daughter that was just what she needed. She saved my family in a way that I know that God sent her to that hospital. That's why I have to help her," Margaret spoke with so much gratitude.

"We definitely thank you. So we won't tell that you helped us. We also made a decision not to tell Kenali either. She doesn't know that we almost found Christian." Lane was letting Margaret know what she did for them was undercover but she has to keep a secret too.

After looking at the puzzled look on Margaret's face, Simbol had to step in to clarify what Lane was saying.

"With her raising a newborn, we didn't want her to be worried about all the things that are going on. If we told her that we found him, lost him plus all of these extra charades it would stress my sister out to the max."

"I understand. She would sit there crying sometimes about your mom's passing. It was like she wanted to show the world that she was strong but on the inside in her private times she held a hurt...oh Jesus. I just had to pray for her."

"That's just how my sister is. She tries to keep a smile on her face so others will be strengthened."

"Well I got to get home. I hope that this helps you find Christian. Be sure to kiss that precious baby for me," Margaret smiled.

"I will and thank you so much for all that you've done."

Embracing Simbol, Margaret patted her on the back while looking at Lane. "You're welcome. Everything is going to be alright."

And then Lane blurted out something that had just erupted in his mind like a volcano.

"Is she pregnant? I just can't get over the pregnancy claim by the person that most recently seen her."

Lane and Simbol anxiously awaited her answer.

"In my opinion, no. She wasn't showing neither did she have the look," Margaret answered with assuredness.

"The look?" Simbol asked out of extreme curiosity mixed with slight confusion.

"I used to be a midwife and it was a glow that any lady that was pregnant had whether she was a few weeks or a few months. It's not scientific. Just something that I picked up from the trade. But it hasn't failed me yet."

As soon as Margaret's car disappeared into what was becoming night, Lane's mind brightened up.

"First of all, Kerry couldn't take care of Christian while Kenali was there because she would have recognized her from New York. Secondly, she wasn't pregnant like our little friend said at the rehab. What's really going on? Let's go to the rehab to see if this lady on this picture is the one that is escorting Christian around. If she is, that opens up a whole new can of worms that I'm ready to squash."

# CHAPTER 19

"Are you two having a good time?"

Kenali looked from Jamal to Shakenda as they lounged around on the floor. They had been the perfect company that afternoon. They definitely helped Kenali keep her mind off Christian. Although she wanted to think about him, after having a baby, she just didn't have the energy to do so. She just had to trust in God that everything would be alright.

"Yes ma'am. I'm having a great time," Shakenda quickly replied.

"I guess you're pretty cool to hang out with for an old gal." As soon as Jamal said it, he braced himself by clutching harder to the pillow that he was already resting on while lying on the floor. And just like he knew it would happen, he felt the weight of a large pillow hit him in the back.

"I've warned you already," Kenali snickered.

"I don't think that you're old. We always thought that you were cool and on our level when you would come to the center," Shakenda came to Kenali's defense.

"Thank you. I won't throw anything at you, Sweetie." Kenali cut a fake mean eye at Jamal who was now looking back at her. Then she licked her tongue out at him.

"Now I know why that gets on Aunt Simbol's nerves when you do that. It's the attitude behind the action plus she can't get to you like she wants to."

"If it gets to you, then let me do it in slow motion. I tell you what I'll record it and text it to you so that you can see it anytime that you feel lonely," Kenali playfully laughed. She hadn't had this kind of fun in a while. Neither had she really laughed like this.

"I meant to tell you that my auntie is nutty but you should have already known that from hanging around her. If you didn't then maybe you're just as nutty as she is." Once again he braced himself. This time he got hit with two pillows from two different directions.

"Oh. So you both are just going to double team me cause I'm the only man in the house."

"No, we're ganging up on you because you say things that you shouldn't. And you shouldn't be talking about your auntie like that. You skating on thin ice," Shakenda warned him with a crooked smile on her face.

"Puhlease. Ya know I lub me some Kenali King. We down like fo flat, Shawty."

"Oh Lord. That's what they're teaching in school now? Interesting."

The three of them laughed at Kenali's look of disbelief and comical dryness. Then Shakenda dismissed herself to go to the bathroom. Kenali was now free to ask him some questions but Jamal beat her to it.

"So what do you think about her?" Jamal asked.

"I've always thought that she was a nice young lady. What about you?"

"She's the type that'll have my back. It's like she expects me to be me. You know."

"So how much have you told her about what's going on?"

Jamal had the look on his face as if he really didn't want to talk on that subject but he answered anyway.

"She doesn't know everything but that I skipped out. I didn't give too many details and she didn't keep pushing me to tell."

"Like I'm doing now?"

"That's right," Jamal quickly replied.

"I'm just trying to get you to talk about what's going on so that you can get it out and get over it. And if you can talk to her or whoever you feel comfortable with about it, then you need to do so. Ok?"

"Ok. I'll talk to you about it when we get back from taking her home. Now I'm just going to clear my head and enjoy right now. You know?"

"I know," Kenali's reply was from a place of being there. She definitely understood that Jamal wants to enjoy the moment.

By the time they finished their conversation, Shakenda was reentering the room to snuggle right back into her same spot. As soon as she sat down, Kenali's alarm went off.

"Be right back."

Kenali hopped up off the couch to disappear down the hallway that led to her bedroom. Then she came back with a bottle and a pacifier that was for medication dispensing to babies. Gathering a sleeping David into her arms, she cradled him just right and then put the dispenser in his mouth. He then began to instinctively suck on it. Jamal and Shakenda was watching with questions in their mind which spilled over to Jamal's lips.

"Auntie, what's that?"

"It's his medication."

"What he taking it for?"

"To control seizures. The doctor told me that if I give him his medication in a timely order that it would lower his episodes until he can grow out of them. That's why I have a timer set for the morning and the evening."

"What causes seizures?" Jamal asked.

Before Kenali could answer, Shakenda answered from a place of great familiarity.

"They don't know. But taking the medication does keep down the occurrences."

"What are you a doctor or something? You didn't put that on Facebook as your occupation. I really don't know you at all," Jamal joked.

"Whatever. I have seizures but I haven't had one in over a year. The doctor said that I may have grown out of them but to keep taking my meds anyway," Shakenda shared with them as if it were nothing.

"How often do you take it? And how does a seizure make you feel? I'm just curious to know what he feels when he has one," Kenali asked with a great amount of concern for both Shakenda and David.

"Once a day. I don't like having seizures because during the attack I black out but afterwards I have a major headache, be tired and my entire body would be sore. The kids used to pick at me at school. They would call me names and ask when I was going to flop around again so they could put it on YouTube. People can be really mean even if you can't help what's going on." Shakenda's look saddened.

"That's terrible that they would say something like that. The doctor said that it was rare for babies his age to have seizures. So I appreciate you for letting me know how it feels. To see him have one and not be able to do anything is really scary for me but at least I know to give him extra special care afterwards just in case he feels like you did."

Jamal was now looking at Shakenda in awe. He couldn't believe how easily she shared that secret. In his mind there was no way that he could open up like that in front of people. Then the thought hit him about what his aunt had said about opening up to get over it. Could he do it? He knew that he wasn't ready to do so with Shakenda but he would open up to Kenali.

"Well, I don't want to be the bearer of bad news but we gotta go. We promised to have Shakenda home at 8 and I don't want her mom to be mad at me for having her late," Jamal announced.

"Awwww. That's so sweet." Kenali was acting as if she was having a Hallmark moment.

"What is?" Jamal questioned. He was clueless.

"What you said. Shakenda let me interpret what he said. What he really said was that he had a really great time with you today and wants your mom to let you come back again."

Shakenda laughed on the outside but on the inside she hated that she shared with him about her seizures. He was now looking at her funny just like the other people from school. Now he was trying to rush her out of there.

Kenali disappeared with David to get him ready to go but Jamal lingered around in the room with Shakenda.

"Thanks," Jamal said.

"For what?"

"You helped my auntie out a lot when you told her that. You got guts girl."

"Are you gonna continue to look at me funny like you did after I said it?"

"I didn't look at you funny."

"Yes, you did," Shakenda quickly replied back.

"No. I was thinking about something that you gave me the nerve to do. Like I said. You got guts. I appreciate it."

Shakenda was relieved. By the time that she reached her front door with Jamal by her side, she didn't want to go in. She was afraid that her mom would ruin a perfect day. She almost kissed Jamal goodbye until the porch light popped on and the door flung open.

"Hey, Ms. Mead," Jamal nervously greeted her. She really caught him off guard.

"Where's your aunt?" She sharply shot back.

"She's right there in the car."

"I can't tell. You probably been riding around all day with my daughter without your aunt."

Before Jamal could say anything else, Kenali yelled out the window as if she knew what was going on.

"Hey Ms. Mead. Thank you for letting Shakenda spend the day with us. Have a goodnight."

"Goodbye," Ms. Mead abruptly said. Once again she had to drop her attitude since she was proven wrong.

Then Jamal walked back to the car already figuring out what he wanted to say in his head. He was going to get it out of his system once and for all.

"Was she giving you a hard time?" Kenali snickered at the thought of Jamal catching it every time he wants to see Shakenda.

"Yep." Then Jamal took a deep breath. "I want to go to the prison to see him."

"What?" That was the only word that would come to Kenali's lips. She knew exactly what he was talking about.

"I want to go see the man that made the donation that got me into this world."

"Why?"

"I have questions."

"Why can't you ask your mom? Are you sure you want to do that?"

"Mom can't answer these questions. She's not him and doesn't know him. I'm sure. I've been wanting to ever since I found out." Jamal was looking straight ahead into the windshield as if a script was scrolling on the surface.

"Have you told her?"

"No. She won't understand. She's going to only try to talk me out of it. I mean it's not like I want to bond with him or anything."

"I'll talk to her to—"

"No. You can't tell her. She won't let you take me."

"And there might be a good reason why. She knows more about him than we do."

"She's afraid of him. But I want to face the fears for her. Please, Aunt Kenali. It's something that I gotta do. I really need your help on this one. Please."

"I really have to think and pray on this one. She's your mom and I would be going against her wishes. This is hard."

"Just sleep on it," Jamal pleaded.

The rest of the ride home was one of the longest rides ever. She could not believe that he had sprung such a request on her. Kenali could understand why he wanted to go see that man. But by not telling Divine what she was doing, she would be stepping over some serious boundaries that shouldn't be crossed. This was going to be a long night. Hopefully her father's answer to sleeping on a matter would work out in the favor of them all.

# CHAPTER 20

"Yes! That's her!" Fran shrieked.

"But you said that she was far along in her pregnancy," Simbol interrogated now like a pro.

"She was. Or should I say is?" Fran shook her head from side to side, exhaling before she started again. "She was very far along and it is possible that she could be having the baby any day now."

"See what we don't understand is that someone that saw her a month ago said that she wasn't even pregnant."

Lane and Simbol watched Fran's different emotions as she internalized the new information that just wasn't fitting with what she saw. Then as if someone had turned on a light inside of her head, her face lit up and her finger swiftly rose into the air in an 'aha' moment.

"I saw this on a soap opera once." She began walking back and forth with her head down reading the words on the floor that only she could see. Then when she looked up again Fran translated her own thoughts. "She's faking her pregnancy. It's all coming clear now. What if she is pretending to be pregnant to make him think that she is your sister?"

"But didn't you say that you think that he has amnesia? He wouldn't remember my sister anyway," Simbol interjected.

"On the contrary. He could have selected amnesia and if your sister was talking about her pregnancy to him while he was in a coma he could remember her saying that without knowing what she looked like. He heard but didn't see her. Those are his freshest memories. And when someone shows up pregnant, he could just assume that this is the one that was talking."

"But that works on TV but how can that work in real life?" Lane's mind wasn't ready to accept Fran's theory since it was so sci-fi to him. He just wanted to know straight forth what was going on without this craziness being a possibility. "And plus why would someone do something like this?"

"On the soap opera, the lady faked it because she was in love with the man and she was trying to trap him," Fran gave her explanation.

Lane really wasn't ready to accept that. Julia was more than enough proof that people could be psychotically in love with someone. And she was dead. There was no way that there could be two people like this in the same man's life in a year's time. Nobody was that unlucky.

Simbol expressed verbally what he was thinking. "These crazy chics seem to be coming out of the woodwork for Christian. I didn't think that lightning struck twice in the same place."

Of course Simbol had to explain the entire Julia situation to Fran. After hearing the story, Fran's mouth was wide open in disbelief. She blinked twice and started once again on her excited rambling.

"Talk about art imitating life. I saw that on another soap opera which answers your first question. Now all we have to do is get down to the why. I hope that it's not like on the shows taking six months for everything to come full circle."

Lane and Simbol looked at each other with the same hopes. They didn't know if they could take another six months of this. Even greater, they knew that they could not hold this type of information from Kenali that long.

# CHAPTER 21

"I just don't want him to go and that's that! He's still my son and that's my decision," Divine seethed.

"You don't have to get upset. I'm just trying to help him," Kenali defensively shot back.

"Taking him to see that monster isn't going to help him any."

"What if it could? Can you even understand how he feels not knowing who he is?" Kenali paused to soften her tone. "I can understand that you don't want to see the man yourself but what if a conversation would let Jamal out this cage that he's been in since he read the letter."

"No! And that's my final answer." Divine was finished.

Kenali could not believe how stern her sister was being. She was accustomed to this type of conflict with Simbol but this was her big sister Divine who had never even raised her voice at anyone as far as she could remember.

"Divine, I don't think that I like you talking to me like this."

"Stop barking up this tree then, Kenali because I don't like having to talk to you like this either."

"Well answer this one last question and I won't ask you anything else about it."

Divine sighed so loudly that Kenali heard it crystal clear through her earpiece. The sound was though they were in the same room. She had to ask since it seemed as if there was something imprisoning Divine as well.

"I'm waiting."

"Ok." Kenali cleared her throat. She had to make this effective especially since Divine would definitely hold her to her word of this being the last question. "If you know that Jamal's being torn apart from the inside out because he's not allowed to seek after the answers that he needs then why did you bring him into this world because he was bound to find out the truth one day? That's like punishing him for having the wrong DNA."

"That was more than one question and a comment. So I think that I'll be hanging up now." Divine's fury was escalating.

"Don't you hang up on me. I'll tell Daddy," Kenali childishly interjected. It was the only thing that she could think of.

"I'm grown. And married. And have children," Divine reminded Kenali.

"Ok. That doesn't work on Simbol anymore either but Divine why would you not want him to know the answers that could free him?"

Divine became stiller than calm waters. She was so quiet that Kenali almost thought that she had really hung up on her. Then she heard the faint sniffles.

"I'm sorry, Divine that I pushed you to this place," Kenali apologetically stated.

"He wants me to forgive him." Divine inhaled and exhaled traumatically. "That monster wants me to forgive him for what he has done to me before he's executed."

"Oh my God," was the only response that Kenali could render.

"When he sent that letter it was like I could feel his presence in the house with me. I got so scared. No one else was there. So I left the letter to run upstairs to find somewhere to hide. It felt like I had been attacked all over again."

"Oh, Divine."

"I had never planned on Jamal finding out. That was one thing that was going to the grave with me. I already have to look at the scars from the bullet holes every single day. Now this man has come and messed up another part of my life again."

"He can't hurt you anymore. He's behind bars. And how did he know where you lived? Don't answer that. It's not like everybody's business is safe and secure online."

"But what I don't understand is how he can ask me to forgive him after what he did to me. He almost killed me. Actually he murdered me. That felt so awful being at the trial with my stomach poked out because I was carrying what belonged to him. And he wants to ask me to forgive him. He can rot in hell for all I care. I will never forgive him," Divine spoke through anger now.

Kenali could feel the sharpness of her big sister's words as cold metal piercing her own skin. She knew that with the state that Divine was in now, asking any further about Jamal going to the prison would be a waste of her breath not to mention completely inappropriate. Her sister was hurting and there was nothing that she could do to help ease that pain. So she sat silently holding the phone as Divine sobbed and vented. Then after a few moments, Divine started to ask questions that were unexpected.

"So do you really think that it would help Jamal to go?"

"I think that he would be able to find some closure. Besides, if it's in his head that it would help then only he knows what he needs to heal," Kenali said.

"You know I can't take him, right?"

"Yes, I know. I can take him. It's no problem."

"I could ask Gerald but I don't know how that would make him feel."

"I think that Gerald would understand but I know someone that works at the prison that I need to see."

"Please don't let this be the wrong thing that I'm allowing. Promise me that you'll take care of him." There was desperation in Divine's voice.

"You're doing the right thing. I promise that I'll take care of him like he's my own," Kenali's voice was soft in reassurance.

"Oh God, help me to understand why this is happening to me," Divine pleaded as she hung up the phone.

Kenali couldn't help but to think about how many times she had asked that question about her own situation. She was getting to the point of understanding that all things she wouldn't understand. If she could just hold on in spite of then she would be better off. Some days were easier than others.

The funny thing is that with her being a motivator, she had no one to really motivate her. She had no one to talk to. So Kenali did what most writers do; vent to the paper through the pen.

Now that Kenali had crossed one hurdle with Divine, she didn't want to press her luck. She wanted to talk to her about the power of forgiveness. That would have to be another topic for another day. Kenali even dismissed the thought that forgiveness was the hold up with her and Christian.

For now, she went to make some phone calls into the penal system to see how she could get Jamal's request granted. Then afterwards, she looked into his fearful eyes as she told him what day that they would be going to visit that man, as he called him, that made the donation to get him here.

# CHAPTER 22

"Lane, at what point do we get the police involved? This woman has clearly abducted Christian," Simbol was dramatic in her speaking.

"Yeah, I already tried that. They said that he can't be considered a missing person since he's moving around on freewill."

"Did you tell them that he has amnesia and is being wheeled around by someone that might not be operating in full mental capacity?" Simbol's tone escalated.

"I like your wording. And yes I did tell them that he might be in the hands of a crazy person. All they said was that we have to prove that he has amnesia and didn't just run off with the lady when he woke up. They said that it happens more often than we know about."

"Really?" Simbol was dumbfounded.

"Yes. The officer said that sometimes a man skips out on his wife with another woman without telling her a thing. And when they find him, he just says that it was over and he's not going back. The problem with our situation is that Christian and Kenali are not married. Plus I think that I said too much. I should have said that we had no clue where he was instead of that he's with this woman."

"You know what?" Simbol questioned.

"What?"

"When I see your cousin again, we're going to have a long spiritual talk in which I'm going to explain to him about the wrath of God versus the wrath of Simbol. God has mercy. And Christian better have amnesia."

"Sounds like you're going to hem Christian up."

"He doesn't call me Ms. Sassy for nothing. He knows how I can be about my baby sis." Simbol was getting irritated.

"I think I'm going to have a talk with him also," Lane stated.

"Oh yeah. About what?"

"How he has us out here being detectives instead of newlyweds. But I do like that feisty side of you that's coming out. I think it's turning me on." Lane winked his eye and licked his lips playfully.

Simbol got closer to her husband and whispered in his ear in a soft seductive manner. "Well you can call me *Mrs.* Sassy then."

With a full grin on his face, Lane pushed all the drama that was going on with Christian to the back of his mind so that he could focus wholeheartedly on the wife that God had given him.

# CHAPTER 23

As Kenali entered the gate, she took in many of the surroundings as did Jamal. His head turned robotically while his eyes focused on everything from the signs with the rules of the prison on them to the razor sharp barbed wire fences. He knew that whoever was in here was meant to stay.

"Jamal, are you alright?" Kenali softly asked. If he said that he wasn't she would without question turn around and get him out of there as fast as she could.

"I'm cool. Just a different feel from what you see on TV." Jamal never stopped looking around. The yard had his attention imprisoned.

"I would understand if you didn't want to go any further. We can always turn around." Kenali just wanted to put that out there so that he would know that he was not obligated. He always had the option of changing his mind. But she knew him too well. There was no way that he was going to turn around now.

"No. I'm good. I gotta do this."

Kenali didn't further respond because she was at the gate now handing papers and identifications to the officer. Then the officer further instructed her which way to go yet Jamal never heard a word. His focus was on the many prisoners that were outside. He subconsciously was trying to pick out the individual that could have done such a monstrous act towards his mom.

Anger was building up on the inside of him like he had never experienced before. There was no fear for entering into this strange place but pure unadulterated anger. If he could hurt this man in some kind of way, he would feel better. After looking at the situation, this man was indeed about to get what he deserved; death.

Jamal was angry that the state did away with the electric chair. He would have wanted to see him fry in Yellow Mama. When they learned about the execution styles in school he thought that it was cruel but now after this man had ruined his life he felt like it was necessary.

As he was being patted down, Jamal made up his mind that he never wanted to be an inmate. Considering the violation that he felt just from being checked out was enough to settle that. He never wanted to be amongst the ones that had their hands hanging outside of the bars barking rude comments to beautiful women like they were doing to his aunt Kenali. No never. This may be a part of his DNA but not his mindset. He would not hurt people like that man did.

They were seated at one of the tables that were in this open room with everyone else. With absolutely no privacy at all, he focused on the door that he had seen other inmates come through. Each time he braced himself asking within if the person that was cracking the seal was the object of his anger.

Kenali looked over at Jamal without saying a word. She noticed that his stare was as cold as the room. If she could see his thoughts she wondered would they frighten her. She herself had some ill feelings toward this person as well. He had almost taken her sister's life although in some aspects he did destroy it. He created an atmosphere of fear that hovered over Divine like a persistent dark cloud. She was no longer carefree. Kenali was so thankful that Gerald was a good man that was understanding and helpful in her healing process.

Kenali seen Jamal's back straighten. She knew that this man must have been on his way over. Kenali didn't know whether to be cordial or give him the same evil stare that Jamal was. She didn't really have time to think about her feelings toward this person since she was so focused on Jamal and Divine's. One thing was for sure, she didn't have to shake his hands. This was a no touching facility although one of the guards overlooked the couple that was seemingly married by the bands that were on their hands when they exchanged gentle pats of emotion.

"You have 10 minutes," The guard firmly stated with a voice that was familiar.

Even his stature was that of someone that she knew. He reminded her of Christian which moved her on the inside. It renewed what she had been suppressing for a while which was the desire to be near him. Kenali played with the thought of Christian being incarcerated being easier to deal with as opposed to being out there without a trace. Once again she had to place him on the back burner of her mind. After all, she was sitting before a rapist, murderer and only God knows what else.

"Hello ma'am. Hello young man. My name is Clark."

He was as gentle as Hannibal from the Silence of the Lambs. There is no way possible that this could be him but Kenali remembered him from the courtroom from sixteen years prior. It was amazing how he hadn't aged much despite what people said about how prison can age and sicken inmates. This man had a peace that surpassed all understanding that she only wished that she had on the outside of these walls. So she spoke back.

"Hello."

Jamal said nothing but he just looked at this man with those same heart piercing eyes. His mouth balled up as if it dared anything nice to come out. Even the guard cut his eye at Jamal briefly in a way signifying that he understood but then he cleared his throat letting Jamal know don't do it. Therefore Jamal felt the need to control his anger so that he could get the answers that he so desperately needed. He skipped over being courteous and went straight for what he wanted.

"Why did you rape my mom?" Jamal spoke dryly.

Clark wiped the peaceful smile off his face to replace it with an all serious look. He had to search his mind for an answer that he had sixteen years to think about.

"To answer that question I would have to go back to the old me that God has delivered—,"

"Skip the psychology. Skip the religious act. Give me a straight answer," Jamal was stern.

Clark licked his lips to remoisten them yet he kept his overall composure of calmness.

"She was so powerful and independent."

Kenali had to interrupt with questions of her own now.

"Did you know my sister?"

"No. It was her persona as she strolled across the parking lot. I had seen her before. She had the same air about her. So I wanted to possess that power and take it away from her."

The answer made Jamal even angrier because it didn't make sense to his sixteen year old mind.

"So you raped her because she was powerful and you weren't. That doesn't make sense. This is garbage."

Kenali had to intervene because she understood.

"Jamal, just let him talk and I'll explain it to you later. Get your answer. Ok."

The guard gave Kenali a look of approval in more ways than one. She had to resist the urge to indulge in his extreme likeness to Christian. She chose to just place a mental sticky note that if she ever needed a replacement for Christian she knew where to find him.

Jamal took her advice, calming himself once again before asking further questions. He was struggling within. In his adolescence, he was dealing with things that he didn't fully understand. All he wanted to do was reach over the table to snatch the very life out this character called Clark. Then he would possess something also. Like father. Like son.

Kenali placed a gentle hand on the back of Jamal's shoulders. The rub was soothing for him.

"So did you get the power that you were looking for? Is that why you tried to kill her?" Jamal asked.

Even Kenali wanted to know the answer to this question.

"No, I didn't. She wasn't like the other women. She didn't display the kind of fear that they did but it seemed as if she was taunting me. So that's why I tried to kill her. That wasn't in the original plan. And why didn't she come with you today?"

Jamal and Kenali both resisted the urge to tell him that he did take her life. Since it seemed as if they would be empowering him in some kind of sick way by giving him such information they had an unwritten code of what not to say. Kenali knew more so than Jamal how that event altered her sister.

"So how did it make you feel when she survived showing how powerful she really was?" Jamal was firing some really wonderful questions for someone that didn't understand fully what was being said by this psychotic man.

"It made me feel like going to the hospital to finish the job but there were guards and family around her all the time.

I kept coming by but couldn't see a way to get to her. I felt defeated. Powerless in a way."

Clark kept on looking into his mind of yesterdays' past. It was somewhat entertaining for Kenali for she recognized when he was doing it. He was coming in and out of the past in which when he was there he fidgeted but when he was the new Clark he was surrounded by peace.

The married couple at the table next to them time had expired. Glancing toward them gave her the opportunity to look at the guard that favored the love of her life so much with longing in her eyes. This wasn't anything sexual but it was a begging of more time. She didn't want to come back into this place again. She wanted Jamal to have everything that he needed today. The guard complied with her silent wish by looking at his watch and then returning back to the same statuesque position that had held him these last ten minutes.

Now she had to step in to rush Clark since his episodes of here and there were slowing down the process.

"What were you like as a child? Were you intelligent?" She asked hoping that Jamal wanted to know that answer.

Clark jolted from one frame of thought to this one which seemed to be pleasant in a painful way.

"Yes. I was very intelligent. I went to a prep school, graduated before time and was in the honor's society. There was a great desire of knowing things that surrounded me. I went to college when I was sixteen. That was about the age you were when I first saw you. You were scrumptious but I wasn't into the pedophile thingy. And once again I'll ask why Divine didn't come today?"

Kenali was caught off guard. His comment molested her. The guard even moved uncomfortably. She had to take control of this situation before an increasingly angering Jamal jumped over the table.

"She had better things to do. I bet your mother was proud of you." Kenali was stabbing at the air to see what kind of relationship that he had with his mom. She had read that rapist were sometimes mentally or physically abused by their mothers.

"I could never please her. Never was I smart enough nor was I good enough. I was into education but she compared me to the sports jocks. Even to this day, I can't say I remember one time that she ever said that she was proud of me. She was a horrible woman and that is the same way that she died." His forehead wrinkled as if he were trying to squeeze out a bad memory. Then he continued. "Oh how I wish that I could see Divine again."

Ignoring his comments about Divine, Kenali asked the already planned questions.

"Why do you want his mother to forgive you?"

This was an answer that Clark knew well. He had studied this one backwards and forwards many times. From a psychological standpoint his answer meant that he was better and had been ridded of his wrongful ways.

"I want to give her the power back."

"But I thought that you said that you didn't take it from her," Kenali shot back.

"In the courtroom, I noticed that I had, which satisfied me greatly. But last year, I was sitting in my cell wondering why I wanted to take the power from her and that if taking power from her was a good thing then why was I being punished. Then I requested some sessions with a chaplain although I never went to church before but it just seemed like I had to. We talked and I finally listened while he told me about forgiveness. He told me that there is power in

SON OF THE FORGIVEN

forgiveness. That this Jesus character, who did nothing wrong, went on the cross so that we may be forgiven. I realized that she did nothing wrong but it was just something misconstrued in my head. So I thought that if she could forgive me then she would be taking back what I stole from her; her power. I know that it will never change anything but it just seems like she won't be living in a hell of hate and fear anymore."

His words moved Jamal to speak because there was something about what he said that he did understand.

"She already has the power back. You thought that you hurt her but she never treated me any kind of way but good. She's always proud of me and tells me that. I would've never known anything about you if you hadn't written. So why don't you leave me and my family alone with these little sick mind control games that you're playing. I'll never be like you. The kind of person that I'll become is already on the inside of me. That's the man that God wants me to be. When you get to hell, tell your mama or should I say grandma I said hey."

Jamal stood up so strongly that the chair scrubbed the floor making a loud screeching noise. It echoed inside this room causing everyone to look their way.

This was a cue for Clark to revert back to his old twisted self. He lost all control. The guard happily restrained him by slamming him face down on the table that he once sat at with so much pretended peace.

There was so much ease in the actions of the guard the entire time he was holding and controlling Clark. He even flashed a smirk at Kenali and then winked at her before dragging this fully grown man out like a screaming ragdoll.

"You little brat, you tell her that I'll finish the job this time. I'm going to get you too, *son*. You all are going to die together."

Although it was something interesting for Kenali to see, she was finally able to take her eyes off that situation to look at Jamal.

"Jamal, how did you know that he was playing mind games?"

"I saw it on TV the other day. The perp tries to control the emotions of the family by playing tricks. That punk is crazy. He's gonna see Jesus alright. But that don't mean he's gonna stay in His presence."

"I'm so proud of you."

"Thanks. I gotta go see my mama and ask her to forgive me. Plus I gotta tell her how you up at the prison flirting with the guard."

Kenali gasped in disbelief. "What are you talking about?"

Ignoring her question, Jamal kept on talking. "He did have the hots for you but you gotta wait on Uncle Christian."

Kenali was elated to know that she had her Jamal back. The young man that had always had wisdom beyond his years had dismantled a crazy man, spotted that a guard felt something for his aunt, and decided that the best choice was the one that was lost.

The two of them walked out the prison with two separate missions on their minds. Jamal had to go find forgiveness for his actions while Kenali's task was going to be harder. She had to find a man that she didn't even know why he disappeared. This visit gave her the power back to do so.

# CHAPTER 24

When they reached the car, Kenali heard her cell phone ringing as soon as she opened the door. She looked at it. It was Divine.

"You must have a hidden camera on us. I'm so proud of your son. He was the bravest," Kenali immediately proceeded as if Divine was anxious to know how the visit went.

Divine abruptly interrupted Kenali.

"David kept having seizures and I brought him to the hospital. We're at Mercy. The doctors have him and they said that he'll be alright."

Kenali was frozen with fear on the inside yet she was making all the moves that would get her to David. She crank the car putting it in motion without a second thought. Kenali didn't even check to see if Jamal was fully in the car. She glanced over to find that he was safely buckled up.

"Which Mercy?" Kenali asked masking the waves of fear that wanted to take over her.

"The one on the south side of town," Divine answered back. She was a mother and knew how worried Kenali must be despite her calm tone of voice.

"We're on our way. It's going to take at least an hour. Divine, is he really alright?"

"I wouldn't lie to you Kenali about this. I drilled the doctors as if he were my own son. They reassured me that all is well. His pediatrician is here and you know that man takes God and Jesus everywhere he goes. That's why you chose him remember? David is in good hands."

"Ok good. I just want to know was he shaking or was he stiffening up."

"He was stiffening up and turning colors. It scared me so bad Kenali that I wanted to start crying. I just tried to be calm as his mommy would be while Gerald drove us to the hospital."

"Thank you both for taking care of my baby. I'll be there as soon as possible. Make sure that he knows that mommy loves him."

By this time Jamal was looking intensely at the side of Kenali's face while she drove. He could figure out from her side of the conversation that something was wrong with his little buddy.

He was no longer concentrating on texting Shakenda, who had been doing so from the time that he told her that he was pulling out his aunt Kenali's garage earlier that morning. She was concerned and he could tell that she was a little frightened for him as well. With his fears being over now he told her about what was going on via a conversation that he was not involved in. He couldn't wait for his aunt Kenali to get off the phone so that he could get full details.

"Ok. Be sure to keep me updated on every little thing, Divine."

"I will baby sis. You be sure to focus and drive safely."

"I will."

As they hung up the phone, Divine was so proud of her sister that she didn't know what to do. She was a full blown mommy now that handled the situation so well. Due to everything that was going on she didn't think it appropriate to ask about Jamal's visit but she would get that information in due time.

"What's going on with lil buddy, aunt Kenali?" Jamal anxiously inquired as soon as Kenali removed the phone from her ear.

"He was having seizures. Your mom and dad took him to the hospital."

Jamal, in all his youthfulness yet with wisdom knew that he needed to encourage his aunt now especially when he could see the tears welling up in her eyes. She tried to be strong for so many people by refusing to show her real emotions. The last time that he saw her cry was at his grandma's funeral. With all the things that are going on with her now even he knew that she was long overdue for a good crying session.

"God is going to take care of him, auntie. Plus he got some of those little fat baby angels flying around to play with him. I heard that their fat was really muscle."

Letting out a snicker, Kenali had to shake her head side to side. She needed that mental break that Jamal was providing.

"Can you ever be serious?"

"Do you need me to be?"

Thinking momentarily about his question, she responded somberly. "No. I don't."

They swapped conversation back and forth which made the longest ride ever emotionally shorter than it would have been if she was riding alone. She pulled into the parking deck. She was walking so fast that Jamal almost was not able to keep up. The click clack of her heels had a rhythm that was speeding up the closer that she got to the elevator.

As she walked across the sky tunnel, she looked out the window to see the busyness of the area in front of the hospital. People were loading into and out of cars. She saw different women going to their cars with babies. Then as she was at the last window before walking into the hospital, she saw a man on crutches standing by a car that looked a lot like Christian. She dismissed it from her thoughts when she saw a woman with a baby come up to him planting a kiss onto his lips. She wished that could have been the welcoming that she received when she had David but it wasn't. Therefore her focus was on providing what her son needed right now; his mommy.

After getting directed to the appropriate part of the hospital, she saw Divine and Gerald sitting in a waiting area. When he saw her, Gerald stood with Divine following his action. Kenali embraced them both.

"Where do I go to see my baby?"

"His doctor came out about 15 minutes ago and told us that when you got here to call him. Follow me." Divine walked swiftly and talked simultaneously.

Kenali followed Divine who when she spotted Jamal shyly standing in a corner passed by him and patted him on the shoulder with a warm smile. They reached the nurses' station asking for the doctor as he had instructed. He came out within a couple of minutes, shook Kenali's hand and gave her some instructions. Then he told her that they did want to keep David overnight for observation. She nodded in agreement.

"When can I see my son?"

"Right now. Don't be alarmed to see the tubes and wires that are connected to him. They are just scanning and recording his vitals to check if he has another episode of seizures. But our little David is going to be alright. He's in the nursery and the nurses will take care of you from here."

"Thank you so much doctor. I'm glad that you came down to check on him."

"Wouldn't have it any other way. God bless you."

Kenali smiled. Then she was led by the nurse that the doctor instructed to let her into the nursery. She followed her around the corner and through a door which even the nurse had to be buzzed into. It slightly reminded her of the prison except this time it was to keep the little ones safe.

"He's right here."

Then Kenali looked down into the face of a baby that was so cute and plump but the only problem was that it wasn't her David. As quietly as she could, she notified the nurse that was now crossing the nursery to go check on other babies.

"This isn't my baby."

The nurse looked with puzzlement before saying his name which was the same as on the name tag as well as the wrist band on his arm.

"I'm sorry. The new nurse must have put the wrong tag on him. Do you mind looking at the other babies to see which one is yours? I'm so sorry you have to do this."

When Kenali got to the last baby, her heart began to beat so loudly. Tension shot up through her neck.

"Is there another area that he might be? None of these babies is my baby."

Shock was all over the nurse's face now.

"This is the only area that we keep the babies in. They have wrist band alarms on so they can't be taken from this floor. Don't worry everything is going to be alright."

Before long Kenali was now talking to the doctor who went to look at the baby that was not the baby that he had checked.

"That's not David. I just checked him a few minutes ago. I know all my babies and have photos with their charts. Lock it down," The doctor ordered with an urgency that exceeded his facial expression. He was trying to remain calm for Kenali's sake.

While the staff and security checked every area of the hospital for little David, Kenali rejoined her family which had grown by three. Her father, Simbol and Lane had now joined the others. Mr. King saw Kenali first and knew that something was wrong.

"Baby girl, what's wrong?"

"Daddy, they don't know where my baby is."

Now Kenali was full of tears. This hospital had never failed to bring her misery. This is the very place that she received the news about her mother. Now under the weight of everything that was going on, she did the same thing that she did on that day almost a year ago; her body went limp in the arms of her father.

After coming to, Kenali was surrounded by staff members and police officers that were saying different things that didn't mean anything to her.

"Don't worry Ms. King. She couldn't have gotten too far away. With the information that your sister and brother-in-law gave us, we'll be sure to grab her before long."

Kenali just sat there numb not knowing what to do, say, or feel. She heard the officer talking but the last thing that she heard was that they couldn't find her baby anywhere in the hospital. The alarm had been placed on the baby that was in David's crib. Right now her hearing was selective. She wanted to hear David's cry coming from down the hall with someone bringing him to her.

"Why is Christian doing this to me?"

"What? Who is Christian, Ms. King?" The police questioned.

"David's daddy. I would know him anywhere. I knew that I saw him outside when I was coming in but I dismissed it when I saw a lady with a baby kiss him. That was my baby."

Kenali was completely still except for her lips. A well of tears flowed from unblinking eyes. She didn't move. She could only watch the memory that was displayed on the wall somewhere across the room. On the inside she felt as if David had been ripped from her womb. Then she closed her eyes and ears to all the noise that was going on. When she opened her eyes, she stood up and walked away.

"Kenali, where are you going?" Divine noticed her cold countenance.

There was no reply. Kenali turned the corner and headed for the elevator with everyone looking at her wondering. Then Divine and Simbol stood up to chase after her. When they got around the corner, she was on the elevator with the doors closing. But they were able to shout out to her asking where she was going. Her reply was simple.

"I'm going to get my baby."

# CHAPTER 25

" I would like to make a plea to anyone that has a heart or just an ounce of compassion. Please help me find my baby. It is believed that he's with this man." Kenali held up a picture of Christian. It was painful for her to look at him. "This is his father who supposedly has amnesia. This woman was his daddy's nurse while he was in a coma and is suspected to be with them. My son David has seizures and he really needs his medication and his mommy's love. Kenali paused to clear the tears that were in her throat. "Please help David come home."

With all of the news reporters that were around her flashing cameras and shoving microphones closer to her, Kenali didn't show any camera shyness. Her only fear at this time would be that she never saw her baby again. She let her tears roll down her face, expressing all of her emotions before millions which was something that she had never done before. This was important.

It had been one month since she had held her son. She couldn't believe how quickly time had passed. It seemed like it was just yesterday when she gave birth. He was only two months old. They didn't have enough time together.

Despite Divine's constant apologetics, Kenali never regretted one bit taking Jamal to the prison. There he was able to get the help that he needed. Divine kept saying that if she would have been strong enough to face her fears on her own then none of this would have happened. Kenali kept trying to let Divine know that she didn't have any blame in her heart towards her. It wasn't her fault.

Kenali was thankful for the information that Lane and Simbol had found. She wished they would have let her known sooner. Lane's reasoning was sufficient. All the yo-yoing would have made her crazy. If it weren't for what they had found out they wouldn't have a clue as to where to look.

Knowing that David was with his daddy did make it a tiny bit easier to deal with. Yet every time she had to use the breast pump to relieve the pressure that David would have by feeding, that ease was altogether deleted. She had to search as if he was in the hands of a complete and total stranger in which one of the culprits were.

Jamal, whom Divine had released to stay with Kenali during this time, was a large help. Without Kenali knowing, he had set up pages on all the social media sites plastering photos of David, Christian and Kerry. He had gained thousands of followers all over the country which brought hope that someone was going to see them. He was posting, tweeting, and whatever else he could do day and night. Kenali really didn't know what she would do without him.

"You still up?" Kenali asked as Jamal still pecked away at the keyboard of the computer.

"Yes." Jamal was intently working on something that had his attention fully.

"Jamal, you have to get some rest sweetie."

"I can't rest until my little buddy is back home."

"But just like your mom told me, you're not going to be any good to anyone if you pass out from exhaustion."

"And just like you told me one time, if you're passionate about something give it your all because it won't turn you a loose anyway. I can't let it go. It's my fault that David isn't here."

Kenali's eyes widened while she gasped for air.

"No it's not. And I don't ever want to hear that come out of your mouth again. This has nothing to do with you."

"If you hadn't been at the prison with me then you would have been with David."

"And he would have had a seizure causing me to take him to the hospital." Kenali had thought about it a million different ways already. She knew that her being home wouldn't have kept David from having a seizure.

"You wouldn't have taken him to that hospital cause I remember you said that if anything ever goes wrong with you not to take you to that hospital." Jamal was right.

"Look Jamal. If I would have seen my baby having seizures, I would have taken him to the first hospital that I could've gotten too which that would have been the one. The reason that I didn't want to go there is because that's where mama died and it was just too painful. I don't want you going around blaming yourself. You're like a son to me and the last thing that I need right now is you blaming yourself for something that somebody else did. Besides if I had to do it all again I would make the same choice." Kenali was now looking Jamal straight in the eyes with her hands resting on both of his shoulders.

"Oh." Jamal for the first time was at a loss of words. He did feel better knowing all of this but he was still serious about finding David. Besides he couldn't stop right now since he was waiting on an e-mail from someone that thinks they have a pic of this highly sought after trio.

"Well goodnight, sweetie. I got to get some sleep. And you need to do the same pretty soon."

"Ok. Goodnight auntie."

Kenali disappeared back into her room because she felt some tears about to flow from talking about her mom and her missing baby. What she really felt was a burden on her heart. She couldn't figure out why she had to go through so much. She knew that reaping what you sowed was real. She couldn't for the life of her figure out what she had sowed that would make her reap all of this. If that one night of sex was the cause then she would never have sex again. Kenali was in a place that didn't feel good at all.

She actually questioned whether or not it was worth it. Was it worth holding up a blood stained banner to only keep getting hit from every angle? Kenali felt like the God that she loved so much had forsaken her. There were no credible witnesses for her to talk to. She couldn't think of not one person that had been through what she was going through now. Simply, Kenali felt like giving up.

And right at the time that she was about to let go, hope burst through her door.

"I found them, aunt Kenali." Jamal burst through her bedroom with so much force that it scared the tears and a foolish decision from her.

"What?" Kenali knew what he was talking about but she was so discombobulated and ashamed for even thinking about wavering.

"I found them. Come and look. I have a pic of them walking around pushing a baby carriage."

Kenali ran to the computer so fast that she ran out of one of her house shoes. She left its pink fuzziness in the dust of desperation.

"Oh my God. That's Christian." She had to put her hand over her mouth to keep from screaming at the computer everything that she wanted to say to both of the adults. The only thing that she could do was assume that her baby was being pushed in that carriage. In her heart, there wasn't a shadow of doubt that it was David.

"They are in a small town called Skippleton, Arkansas. The person that sent this pic to me said that they have been there about three weeks."

"Will they send you the address?"

"They already gave it to me."

Kenali turned to run into her room leaving Jamal sitting at the computer looking dumbfounded. She emerged in about five minutes fully dressed with a small bag in her hand.

"Quick. Pack your bag. We gotta go."

Kenali sped down the interstate listening at her GPS give turn by turn directions. It wouldn't be relaying any directions for a while since she was on a long stretch of highway that didn't require any turning. With how her heart was racing she knew that she could make a seven hour drive without stopping other than for gas.

She was awaiting a call back from Detective Morris who had phoned the Skippleton Police Department with the address. He said that these things take a little time while he urged her not to go into this dangerous situation not knowing much about the lady. Detective Morris tried his best to get her to turn around to wait for morning to come so they could share in the news together. The only news that she wanted to hear was that they had her son in their possession. She knew that she was going to stand victorious on this day. She was going to do it at the address that housed her David.

"Do you have any children Detective Morris?"

"No."

"Then you're wasting your breath."

"I figured that much. I just want this to be as safe as possible, Ms. King."

"I just want my baby back and I'll get there before they get an order to go do something. I'll call you when I'm holding my son."

Safe was the one word that kept running through Kenali's mind. It was going to be safe alright. As soon as Kenali got David back in her arms she was going to show the teenagers what it meant to go ham on someone. This lady was going to get it and Christian too if Kenali saw any signs that he didn't have amnesia.

# CHAPTER 26

C hristian tossed and turned in his sleep. Sweat beaded up to roll into the hollow part of his neck that sat south of his Adam's apple. There was a fight going on in his unconscious world that caused the very veins in his neck to rise up violently underneath his skin. When he could no longer take this torment, he sprang up as if coerced to do so by some invisible force.

"Are you ok?" His fiancée Kerry, who was lying by his side asked in a sweet understanding voice.

"Yes. I'm fine. Didn't mean to wake you. Go back to sleep." That was the only answer that he could produce that probably wouldn't get him in any trouble. After all, how could he tell the mother of his child, the woman that had nursed him back to health that he was dreaming of two other women? He really wished that he would get his full memory back since he was tired of being anguished by car crashes and funerals in his sleep.

Thankfully these nightmares just started a couple of weeks ago. It would have been very tormenting to be in a coma unable to wake from them. As he sat on the side of the bed, he reached for his crutches so that he could go into the bathroom as quietly as possible so that he wouldn't wake his son. Fortunately, as he looked down into a tiny replica of himself, his son had been unaffected. There was no way that he could deny his son. Even at his young age, he looked so much like him.

Christian rubbed the side of his son's head wishing that he could take the seizure disorder from him. Lying in his crib he looked as if he had never been affected by anything. But when Kerry came out the hospital with their son that day, he was so proud to be his father. It was the first time that he got to see him since he was born because of his seizures and Christian's own inability to maneuver around.

He knew that Kerry had to be a strong woman. She was so busy trying to see to his every need while running back and forth to the hospital to visit their newborn son. She had that same routine for almost a month. And now Christian was dreaming of other women.

When he got into the bathroom, he propped both crutches on the edge of the medicine cabinet while he put the weight of his 6'4 250-pound frame onto the sink. Even though he couldn't remember what kind of place that he had before, he surely hoped that it was better than this. He didn't complain since Kerry had been taking care of them on just her income alone.

The leaky faucet that he looked down at was the cause of the rust stain inside of the pale pink basin. He looked at the outdated pink tile that was everywhere and made a declaration that he would get better as soon as possible if not earlier. He refused to raise his son in such an environment. He wanted his son to have a backyard of grass and trees to play in not the current yard of dirt that had a few sprigs of weeds here and there that were just waiting to be choked out by the surrounding dirt.

The more he thought about it, the small one bedroom apartment looked very closely to an old two story hotel that had been remodeled probably sometime around the time he was born thirty-five years ago. He dismissed its décor from his mind since it was only temporary living quarters due to it being close to one of the best rehabilitation facilities in the country according to Kerry. After all, she was a nurse who seemed to know her stuff. Therefore he left those complaining thoughts alone.

As he revisited the thought about his age, he was thankful that things such as his name and date of birth were on his medical record. All the other things he knew were due to his fiancée telling him. Had she not been there to fill in the gap, he didn't know where he would be. Even still, there were things that she couldn't answer. Body wise he had made a lot of progress since he had been out of the coma. He was just waiting for his mind to catch up.

"You gotta get better. Now!" Christian pounded his fist on the edge of the sink. This was his way of encouraging himself as he could hear a female voice saying, 'be in good health even as your soul prospers'. Outside of that phrase the only other thing that he remembered was a name which was the first thing he said when he woke up. *"Kenali."*

It was nights like these that made him push harder and harder. When he looked at the mirror, he could see the scars that would always be there as proof that part of his nightmare was real. What he couldn't figure out was the funeral. It was the funeral of an older lady that he guessed was his mom but there was this beautiful woman that was crying in his arms. Maybe that was Kenali.

Then there were the scenes that weren't anywhere near nightmarish unless he was talking in his sleep. He would kiss and make love to her leaving him to feel something deep within for her. Christian felt this even when he was awake as if she was real which caused him to feel guiltier. Even his dreams chastised him. As soon as they were happy together, he would dream of the other woman that drove them over the cliff. Just the falling without control was enough to catapult him out of fantasy land.

Christian looked into the mirror one last time on this night as if he was commanding his memory to return. Just like every other night, it didn't. He would do what he had done all the other nights; go back to lie down beside his fiancée, the mother of his child wishing that he wouldn't selfishly dream about another woman that was just a figment of his imagination. After all, if he was man enough to propose to this woman and man enough to get her pregnant then maybe he was man enough to be happy with her.

But tonight he needed some rest for his early morning therapy session would soon be here.

# CHAPTER 27

The sun had just been up for a couple of hours when the GPS gave its last set of directions. She couldn't believe that she was this close to her baby.

*'Your destination is on the right.'*

She knew that its final direction was true when she saw the three police cars outside of the house. Her heartbeat must have loudly increased since Jamal abruptly came out of his sleep. She couldn't wait to hold David again. Now only being steps away from him, she threw the car in park and was out the door, leaving it wide open. She was moving faster than her thoughts.

"Ma'am, can we help you?" One of the officers said with a real deep southern drawl.

"I'm the mother of the baby that was kidnapped. I just got here to get my son." Kenali was talking but she was looking around this man to see if one of the other officers was carrying him.

"You're Ms. King?"

"Yes." Kenali was annoyed at him blocking her.

"Well, we thought that you were going to wait in Alabama for our call. The family isn't here right now. We figured that we would wait until they got home so that we could ask them some questions and ID the baby."

Kenali paused. She couldn't believe what she heard. Even she knew that was not going to happen. She tried to calm herself so that she wouldn't say the wrong thing but Jamal beat her to the punch.

"What kind of kidnappers comes back when they see police cars everywhere? Just saying!" Jamal was sarcastic but true.

After Jamal made the statement the officer looked dumbfounded proving that they were in a really small town that never dealt with any kind of serious crime. She could not believe that Detective Morris wanted her to leave her baby's safety in the hands of these hick town police. Kenali was infuriated at the fact that the officer had nothing else to say and when he did it wasn't any better but it was helpful.

"Well Ma'am, the neighbors said that they left early this morning possibly taking the man to rehab and that they'll be back soon."

Kenali lost it.

"They're not going to come back if you're here," she screamed at the top of her voice through clinched teeth. "I have come too far to get my son and you better not screw it up."

Her voice made everybody stop dead in their tracks. The other officers came over as if they were going to assist their fellow officer until she let them have it also.

"What?! Who came up with the idea to bring three squad cars to a place and wait for the kidnappers to show back up? If I don't get my son back today, it's going to be trouble in the land."

Kenali was dialing so fast that it beat human possibility. She was so angry that she was shaking. She wanted to see if Detective Morris was going to agree with the tactics of these three goof troop morons. While she talked with him, she had to walk around with one hand on her hip to keep from bursting a gasket.

"Put one of them on the phone." The way that Detective Morris said those words let her know that she was correct in her thinking. She handed the phone to the first one that she got to since she had the same sentiment towards them all.

After a series of "uh hunh", he handed the phone back to her with damaged pride. Then he went to talk to the other two that stood under a tree far, far away from Kenali. After he said something to them they turned, apologized to her, got in the squad cars and left.

Then she wondered what was going to happen now. Had Christian and that woman already been by to notice that the police had found them out? The only thing that she could do now was pull her car into a place out of sight and pray.

---

*'She is real,'* was Christian's thoughts as he seen her running to talk to one of the officers that was outside of their apartment building. Momentarily he wondered what kind of trouble someone was in that lived around them. He couldn't help but to feel uneasy since this is the very woman that was just a part of his dreams as of last night. Those were the same curves that he held night after night. The same reddish brown skin that he caressed in his dreams.

Christian's mouth dried when Kerry said something about baby's milk that he couldn't hear due to thinking he was about to get busted. Whatever she said, it meant that she was going to pass the apartment and the woman from his dreams which were safe until he could figure out how he knew her. In his heart, he was certain that he had an affair with her. Since the crash was true, why wouldn't that be also?

# CHAPTER 28

"Gerald, do you think that I should go to the execution." Divine was sitting up in the bed talking to her husband.

She was thankful that he had received a promotion to the day shift supervisor at the Mercedes plant which meant he finally would be home at night. With everything that was going on with Kenali and Jamal, she really needed his support right now. Until recently, she didn't know how fearful she really was. When the letter came, that was the bitter icing on the cake.

"Do you feel like it would help?" It was an honest question from an honest man. He was a hard worker that provided for his family therefore being a man of many words wasn't in his character.

"I don't know? But what if it would and I don't go then I'll never know. I mean Jamal was brave enough to go visit and he got better almost instantly."

Gerald came out of the bathroom, dressed for bed in his pajama pants and no shirt. Divine often picked at him that he must have hot flashes although she never grew tired of seeing the line of hair that streamed from his belly button to disappear behind the waistband of his low sitting pajamas. His body was chiseled flawless.

"That was a visitation. This is an execution. It's going to be much different. Regardless, whatever you decide, I'm here for you, baby. There's no need for you to be afraid."

Gerald kissed his wife on the cheek then slid underneath the covers on his side of the bed.

Divine looked down at him as he lied flat on his back with one hand behind his head while the other rubbed up and down his chest. He did that when he was in deep thought.

"Baby, why are you still afraid?" His eyes never left the ceiling.

"I don't know. I guess because you hear about people breaking out of jail all the time. Some of them break out just to finish the job. What he said in the courtroom never left me. It's like a ghost that haunts me all the time." Divine now leaned her head back onto the headboard so that if Gerald did look he wouldn't see the amount of fear that was actually there.

"So have you thought about forgiving him?"

Gerald's question made Divine tightly squeeze her eyes shut. She had been so confused about what she should do about that since the letter came. Before that, she didn't think about forgiving him. She just always thought that she was excluded due to the circumstances.

"It doesn't matter if I forgive him or not. He needs to ask God for forgiveness." She knew that answer was elementary enough to only provide her an escape for a few seconds.

"You know better than that. He didn't commit this crime against God," Gerald replied.

After a moment, Divine lowered her head to look at her husband who was now looking at her.

"Why do I have to Gerald? Could you if you were in my shoes?" Divine was fighting back tears. Her eyes blinked rapidly. This was so hard for her that she wished that she would have never said anything about it.

Gerald sat up in bed beside her, grabbing her hand in the most compassionate way.

"I couldn't even begin to imagine how you feel. I've tried all of these years, baby. My mind just don't reach that far into pain. All I know is that I've wanted to tell you that you will be alright once you forgive him. It's like our son said. It's about power. So show him that you have the power to forgive him. Besides, he's about to die anyway. He won't ever be able to hurt you again unless you allow him to in your mind."

Divine lost the fight to hold back the tears as they were flowing freely now. Gerald did what any good husband would do; he hid her in the safety of his arms. He wanted to shield her from any hurt but it was something about the hurt that she harbored inwardly that endangered her the most.

After she felt that she had released a sizable portion, she wiped her face with both hands.

"You're right. I just got to find a way in my head to let it go. It's eating at me like a cancer. And I got to do this for my family."

So the couple slid down underneath the covers while Gerald held her praying that she did finally stop that monster from bringing fear into his family.

# CHAPTER 29

"Christian, I just figured that you wouldn't mind leaving that dump. I didn't really like that area but now we don't have to move anymore. We can be happy here," Kerry sincerely pleaded with him.

Christian listened to the words that were coming out of her mouth. Although he didn't have his memory he felt like something was wrong. Yet he didn't start feeling like this until yesterday when he saw the lady from his dreams. Somehow, he felt like the only person that could give him some answers was her.

He was so confused. It was something about not knowing who he is and seeing people from inside his head that made his amnesia worse. Kerry really couldn't help him either. He thought that it would be opening a can of worms. Besides he knew that the doctor had told him that it would be best if he just let his memory come without someone else filling it in for him. She reiterated that point to him every time he asked her something. If it wasn't for the doctor's reason, Christian would have wondered if Kerry had amnesia as well.

But there was one thing that was very clear inside of his mind. He was going to find some answers as soon as he got back on his feet literally. He needed to be able to maneuver without the crutches especially since he had the feeling that when he went to start digging he may need his full strength to stand against whatever he found.

Speaking of finding things, he figured that a lot of things could get lost out here where they were. If they had a neighbor, he wouldn't know it. The trees were so dense that light didn't penetrate any area that wasn't already cleared out. He just stared out the window looking at their new habitation. One good thing is that he did want a yard for his son to play in once he got older. Now he had plenty; as far as the eye could see.

"I hope that you're not disappointed." Kerry's voice pierced his thoughts in such a way that he had to replay what she said to respond.

"It's great. This is a wonderful place for our son to grow up in. I would say that I grew up somewhere like this but I don't remember." Christian just dropped his head.

She strolled across the room, first placing a hand on his back then wrapping him completely in her arms. His mind was in her hands.

"As soon as you get better, then we can take trips back home to see if you remember anything. I know you will. But remember to just let it come naturally." Kerry squeezed him tighter which gave him hope.

After all, she did just give birth to their son. He figured that taking care of the both of them was like having twins. At least now, they were all under the same roof relieving her of the taxing duty of running from the hospital to the rehab to check on the both of them. He knew that it must have been hard on her leaving David in the hospital after birth. He wished that he could have been there for that also.

Kerry was right about him needing to get better to take trips. Although he knew it, when she said it, it opened up something in him that made him even more determined to make his weakened, stiff legs work faster. Kerry's words mixed with the realness of the beautiful woman from his dreams became a driving force for him. Maybe he will see her again while he is alone so that he could lather her with question after question until she satisfied his psyche.

He patted Kerry's hand signifying that he was alright.

"Thanks. I'm going to go outside to take in some of this wonderful fresh air."

She released him. "Ok. Be careful."

Christian made his way down the steps of the front porch without error. Steps were tricky especially these wooden steps that creaked and slightly swayed underneath his weight. Sensibly he tried to hold onto the crutches and the hand rail as an added safety measure.

It was quiet everywhere. He kind of liked it. He decided to venture cautiously into the woods. He fed off the strength of nature. The unevenness of the ground helped him to focus on stabilizing himself. By the time that Christian reached the trees, he was exhausted.

Looking through them he saw a small body of water that he would certainly strive to reach as it would be a peaceful place to think. Leaning temporarily on the tree he told himself to go for it. The brush on the ground with all of the pine combs and fallen sprigs would be worse than where he had just come from. In his mind he heard his physical therapist saying to be sure not to reinjure his leg. It would surely be a setback. However, he knew that if he stopped now it would be a mental setback. The water was calling him.

From the last row of the trees, he truly could say that the grass was greener on the other side. The trees gave way to allow the sunlight to grace the water. Since it was a slope,

Christian decided to use the tree to get on the ground to crawl to the water's edge.

He felt accomplished as he sat there with his feet only inches from becoming wet. Focusing on the imaginary boundary that kept the water from reaching him, his mind flashed a new memory of her that involved water. He shook his head from side to side because he didn't want to taint his memory with fantasy.

Although he didn't want to, Christian allowed himself to be consumed by what was playing behind his eyes regardless of if it were real or not.

They were dancing by the water's edge, holding one another in the dusk of the day. She was looking up at him with such love in her eyes. Her fit was perfect in his hands. It was as if they were made for each other. He saw lights hanging in trees and candlelight underneath the gazebo where it looked as if they had just finished dinner. He could almost feel his appreciative emotion intensify as they danced. She smiled at him.

"Christian!" Kerry desperately called crashing his thoughts.

"Yes," he sluggishly answered almost wishing to be invisible.

"You didn't hear me calling you?"

Christian wondered how deeply involved was he with his daydream that he half prayed was a real memory.

"No. I didn't." His voice was dry as sand but he decided that he needed to shake himself from that mood. "I guess I was so focused on seeing a fish or something that I couldn't hear."

"It's ok. I was just checking on you. Don't you think that it's a bit dangerous for you to be way out here by yourself? What if you fall?"

"I'll be alright."

"You remember what the therapist said about—"

"Sudden moves and falling. I know. I know. I know." Christian smiled handsomely to one side. His laugh lines on that side of his face was displayed in such a playful way that no woman in her right mind would get mad at anything that he said before the smile.

She returned his smile in a way that let him know that she was serious.

"Well. I'm going back into the house to check on your son. Don't be out here too late."

"I see the nurse is making her rounds. And I won't be much longer."

After Christian watched her disappear through the trees, his mind went back to his memory but this time differently. He halfheartedly wanted to ask Kerry if the name Kenali meant anything but he was afraid that it might spark something that he couldn't handle at this moment.

He also wondered why and how he could remember the two other women in his dreams but he had not once had a flash of his own fiancée. He pondered that if she knew him so well then why hadn't she popped into his mind. They knew each other enough to create a baby together yet the times that stuck in his blank mind were when another woman was in his hands.

And what did she mean by, *"Your son"*?

# CHAPTER 30

D ivine sat cementingly quiet behind the glass wall. This was the only thing that seperated her from the man who monstrously seperated her from herself. But now she was a free woman.

She looked over at Gerald who was glaring at the process of the workers connecting all the wires and straps to this apparently disturbed person. Clark demanded electrocution over lethal injection. Yellow Mama, the nickname given to the state's electric chair, would be the last to hold him. After talking to him earlier, Gerald and Divine both knew why he had made that decision.

Divine couldn't believe how much strength that she had as she sat across the table from Clark, the man that stole her carefree spirit. She had lived in a living hell for sixteen years until she made her final decision just a few short days ago.

"I forgive you," she truthfully said.

The criminal side of Clark was shocked at how firmly she held her composure. He was expecting Divine to emotionally break down grabbing onto her husband for support. But she didn't. Divine looked so much like that proud, bold, powerful woman that he set out to destroy all those years ago. Clark's eyebrows wrinkled at his failure.

"Don't we need to talk first. I need to tell you something." Out of desperation, he tried to make her have a conversation with him.

"It doesn't matter. I've let it go and I forgive you," Divine sympathetically interjected. Her tone was as if she was talking to one of her children when they needed to be reassured about something.

Clark was now squirming. He picked at the exposed mustard yellow cushion foam in the seat. He violently snagged small amounts of it dropping in onto the floor. His plan wasn't working out how he had it in his demented mind. He dreamed for years that it would work out with her being powerless instead Divine was digging her nails into the crevices of his brain. Yet he would try to find a way to tear her down. This was his last attempt.

"How is *our* son doing since he came to visit me?" Clark's nose twitched with arrogance. He needed something to gain leverage. This should have been sufficient.

Divine knew from the first moment that she saw him, coupled with what Jamal told her, that he was going to play that card. She had already prepared. Thank God for discernment.

Pointing to Gerald, "*Our* son is doing fine."

She stressed certain words to make sure that he got the point that there wasn't an *our son* when it came down to him. But he kept on talking as if he failed to receive the point.

"I just didn't want him to feel any weird way knowing that his daddy is dying. A child needs his father even though I can't be there for him. It was really good seeing him the other day. Did he tell you that I asked about you. " A smirk rose upon Clark's face. He felt like levitating victoriously from his chair.

Now Divine was thankful that her son and sister were wise enough to know that he was playing mind games.

"Yes. They told me. But like I said, *our* son is fine. You're not his daddy. He doesn't have your DNA," Divine mimicked Clark's smirk with a coolness that put nails in his coffin.

Divine had him just where she wanted him; shocked and off balance. She wasn't trying to tear this individual up but she was trying to destroy the spirit that operated on him. She couldn't believe that she let this person control her for this long.

"How can he not be my son? That's what you said in court when you were pregnant. They did the test." He had raised his voice slightly. Clark was perturbed. Gerald sat up straight positioning himself to take on Clark if he made the wrong move. The officer had to put his hand firmly on Clark's shoulder reminding him that he would snatch him up in a heatbeat. Clark was outnumbered.

"I had him checked out and the DNA doesn't match," Divine boldly stated. Noticing Gerald's countenance, she felt protected.

Clark was now angered beyond reason. He made the one wrong mistake that allowed the guard to do what he wanted to do all along; drag him out of there effortlessly. The guard didn't appreciate the games that he was playing on this family so he manhandled him all the more.

"You whore!" He screamed repeatedly while being drug out of the room.

Gerald with widened eyes looked at Divine who was powerfully staring at this man who was painfully holding onto the door so much that his knuckles and fingertips were almost tye die; they were streaked with red, yellow and white.

When he was completely gone out of eyesight as well as earshot, Gerald had to know why she had lied.

"Why did you tell him that?"

Divine smiled before she answered.

"I did check Jamal out. He may look like him a little but you are always going to be his daddy. He has your characteristics. God made sure of that. He doesn't have any of that man in him. Our son will not be a serial rapist but he will become whatever greatness that he sets his mind to because he's been changed."

Now, as the straps were being tightened, Clark stared into the one-way glass hoping that he was eyeballing Divine. Before they put the hood over his head, he yelled out, "Look at what you have done to me, you whore! I hope you rot in hell. Rot in hell I say. You and that bastard child!"

The lady on the front row burst into tears assuming that he intended those words for her. She was one of his victims of rape. Divine would have to explain Clark's intent to her afterwards.

She looked at the women that he had tried to destroy by raping them. Yet out of the ones that he wanted to rape and kill, she was the sole survivor. Clark allowed evil to lead him to that dark place and it left him to die alone.

God had prevailed here. Divine truly did forgive him. It was something about when her mind was able to release the pain, fear and agony that she felt so much like her old self again. Gerald was right when he said that she had to forgive in order to be healed.

Her mind went back to an interview that she had with the local paper. The reporter asked her how she had been so successful in the clothing design business. The answer that she wished that she was brave enough to say rolled into her head. She was successful because she felt uncovered and exposed. Therefore as she pieced fabric together, she was hoping that she could sew up that tear in her mind so that she could return back to wholeness. Today, she was whole again.

Clark screamed as his body jolted violently giving purpose to all the straps. She realized, as she turned her head pressing her eyes into Gerald's shoulder, that he chose to die the same way that he lived—violently.

# CHAPTER 31

"You're making a lot of progress since we've been here." Kerry tried her best to motivate Christian. He had been acting distant since they had been there.

Christian didn't even respond. He felt isolated. It had been days since they had been anywhere. Feeling like a prisoner was the only thing that pushed him to work as hard to recover. He couldn't even believe how she said that he didn't have to take anymore therapy sessions.

Not being able to put his finger on it, he still knew that something was wrong with each passing day as Kerry's jumpiness increased. It was almost as if she was hiding something. Before long he was going to know exactly what it is. He had to.

Then, still not speaking to her, he walked into the bedroom to check on his son, as she had put it. He was making sounds signifying that he had woken up from his nap. And since all babies at his age only slept and ate, he knew that it was time for a feeding. He picked him up, looking at his features.

"Yes, you are definitely daddy's baby. Mama's maybe."

That little comment that she had made days ago was still churning in his mind. He figured that a proud mother would say something that would claim ownership of her child not give it away. Christian just kept trying to shake the comment as just a slip of the tongue but it wouldn't let him go.

"It's time for him to eat. Can you bring a bottle?" Christian yelled into the other room. Soon after she followed with his request, handing it to him and preparing to turn to exit the room but Christian had questions.

"Why don't you breast feed our son? I read that it was healthier for him than this milk. You never know. It could help free him from the seizures."

She never even turned to face him but just replied with her back to him. "I can't. My nipples are damaged."

Answering to her back, Christian continued the conversation. "Oh really? What happened? You know I don't remember."

"I attempted to have implants years ago and it didn't quite work out for me." Kerry bit her bottom lip. She still didn't turn to face him.

Christian figured that the answer was either one of two things; the truth or a quick on the feet lie. Before they moved out here he believed what she told him. Now since seeing the woman from his dreams, all the sudden relocations and the cancellation of his therapy, he didn't know what to believe anymore.

Yet as she was going to attempt to walk away once more, he decided that he wasn't finished with his interrogation.

"When was the last time that you fed our son?"

She let out a sigh letting him know that his line of questioning was annoying her. Then she turned to face him before she responded.

"I just gave him a bottle about three hours ago before he went to sleep." Kerry's shoulders drooped when she annoyingly exhaled. She even rolled her eyes in a display warning Christian that she neither had time for this nor appreciated this line of questioning.

Christian totally ignored her actions. He wasn't done.

"No. I mean when was the last time that you actually held him in your arms and fed him?"

Rolling her lips inward as if to trap any profanity that wanted to come out, when she did speak, she was slow to do so.

"Christian, where are these questions coming from?"

"Just asking," he shot back in a way that let her know that he still expected an answer.

"I don't know the exact time but I'm thankful that I have you to help. I've just been so tired lately. My gynecologist told me that I was low on iron which is normal after a woman has a baby. Also, I just thought maybe since you were getting so much better that the two of you would want to bond more." Kerry hoped that her whining helped to get him off her back. She even wondered if he was on to her or if his memory was coming back. After all, he probably did see Kenali when they passed by that day. Kerry hoped greatly that she didn't trigger a memory in him.

Christian felt so crazy and heartless for asking her all of those questions. Looking back over her behavior the last few weeks, how could he not see that she was physically drained?

"I'm sorry. I guess I was being a little insensitive. You just have to pray for me that's all."

She laughed with relief but it didn't last for long before Christian had started again with questions that she didn't feel like answering.

"Hey speaking of prayer, what was that prayer that you prayed to me in the hospital? I remembered it awhile back."

Christian was overjoyed that he was finally able to interject a piece of his memory into their conversation. The look on her face didn't seem to express the same joy. Then she came around.

"That's great Christian. I'm happy for you. Oh my God, I left something on the stove. I'll be right back." Kerry darted out the room in such a hurry that she almost ran into the wall.

While Christian sat there holding the bottle in his son's mouth who was sucking greedily, he strained to gain voice recognition from his memory of the prayer. It was unfolding to him more and more.

Then he jolted to his feet at the same time that Kerry let out a blood curdling scream before he heard a thud hit the floor.

"What's wrong?" He yelled out as he laid his son into the crib.

Then he went into the kitchen as fast as he could on the crutches to see her body lying on the floor. She was moaning while she held her hand close to her chest. Her look was as if she was dazed.

"What happened?" He asked as he used the crutches to kneel down beside her. He reached for her hand but she pulled back from him. Her palm was inflamed.

"I felt faint when I got to the stove. Then I fell and tried to catch myself. I guess I grabbed the wrong thing," Kerry's voice was weak as she explained.

"We need to get you to a doctor," Christian replied.

"No. I'm a nurse remember. I can take care of a burn."

"I can also but that's not why I want you to go. You might need to get your iron checked."

"I'll be ok. It's nothing that they can do anyway. I just have to take the medication they gave me and ride this out until it gets back to normal."

"Are you sure?"

"I'm sure. Thanks for your concern Christian. You're a good man."

Christian, grabbing onto the counter, used his upper body strength to pull them both up. Standing at the sink doctoring on her burn caused him to observe that not only was his memory coming back but he was just as she had said; getting better since they had been there.

----

Christian's mind was doing some great unfolding. In his sleep, the quietest time that he owned, he had more memories of that beautiful woman that he named Kenali. Tonight was no different.

He saw her approaching him in an airport with a look of desperation on her face. He felt as if she was going to tell him something that he didn't want to hear, like goodbye forever. It was the total opposite. She reached out for his hands. The same words she said, he repeated.

"I confess Jesus to be my Lord and Savior. I am saved."

Then he woke up. He lied still for a few more moments before he did his usual routine of trying to quietly go into the bathroom to sort his thoughts. After he got in there, he let the lid down on the toilet, sitting on it completely still allowing the thoughts to keep running through his mind.

This thing was getting weirder to him than he ever thought that it would. Was this amazing looking woman that he had made love to some kind of missionary or something? What kind of person was he before he lost his memory?

What kind of relationship did they have outside of confessing that he was saved?

The thing that really puzzled him was the fact that the feel of the dreams let him know that he was dwelling inside of actual memories. They felt just as real as when he remembered the prayer that he thought his fiancée Kerry was praying to him. So was the one that was praying over him really the woman from his dreams?

His mind resorted back to the place that Kerry looked shocked when he asked her what the prayer was. There was no recognition in her face that let on that she had any clue to what he was talking about. Due to her fainting spell he never did get an answer.

Christian already knew that he wasn't going to get too much out of her anyway so he was going to have to get his answers from the one that he has the most memories of; Kenali, the woman of his dreams. He didn't know her full name even if that was her first name or where to find her. Regardless, he was going to find her along with the answers that he so desperately needed without failure.

# CHAPTER 32

" **J** amal, sweetie. Let's have a talk." Divine had come to the conclusion that she no longer felt the need to hide anything from him especially since he knew.

"Ok," Jamal responded with a quietness that even he wasn't accustomed to.

"With everything that has been going on we never got the chance to talk about you and me or the decisions that I made. I want you to know that I love you so much and that anything that I did was to protect you." Divine bit her upper lip as if she was almost afraid to go on.

"Mama, I know. You don't have to say anything," Jamal compassionately replied since he could hear the tears welling up in her throat.

"No. I have to say this. It's for me. You'll understand one day. Jamal, you're my firstborn, my special child. Although you didn't come the way I would've planned, you got here and I wouldn't trade you for the world. I didn't tell you who your real father was because I was afraid that you might be conflicted within yourself. Then there was the fact that I was afraid to tell the truth since I didn't want to talk about that night ever again. I had so much hate within me." Divine swallowed deeply.

"Do you have to forgive him since he did something so bad to you?" Jamal questioned in all sincerity.

"Believe it or not son, I had to in order to be free. He wasn't the only one that I had to forgive." Divine sighed heavily.

"Who else?" Jamal was wondering who else would be the object of this unforgiveness that she harbored.

"I had to forgive my friend that didn't show up that night. All these years I placed equal blame on both of them. I figured that if she would have been there then this wouldn't have happened to me."

"Why didn't she show up?" Jamal asked with an increasing amount of hate in his voice. Even though he didn't know who this friend was that his mom was talking about, he was mad at her now.

"It's ok, sweetie. She said that she called to let me know that something had come up. But she never did. I found out that she had met some guy on the street, got to talking with him and just blew me off like she had before but this time it backfired. I was so upset with her that I cut off all contact with her until the other day. I figured that if I could forgive the man that did this to me then I could forgive someone that had nothing to do with it. Holding that hatred on the inside was like a cancer eating me up all of these years. And she said the same thing. What I didn't know is that she blamed herself. Now we are both free. And I want you to be free too." Divine looked into Jamal's eyes with such intensity that it was electrifying.

"But I'm still mad at how he tried to play with your emotions." Jamal stood up just like the man that was his real father; Gerald. Divine smiled at his anger.

"You act just like your daddy."

Jamal was offended. "How can you say that I act like that man?"

"I'm talking about *your daddy,* Gerald. He is the one that loved you, raised you, fed you, clothed you, adopted you as his own. He's your daddy. And guess what?"

"What?" Jamal's anger was receding.

"Because you told me what happened when you and Kenali went there, I got some revenge on Clark." Divine smiled for she knew that her son would be happy to hear the news.

"How?" Jamal's eyes brightened up as his mood did also. She had never seen his green eyes that were streaked with brown in such an exotic way so luminous.

"I told him that you weren't his child. Technically you're not." Divine's gesture and smirk on her face made Jamal laugh for real. It had been so long since he was himself. This time was satisfying to her to be able to give him that back.

"Ma, what happened? Don't leave nothing out." He was like the old Jamal that was so close to her. The one that was truly her firstborn.

"He flipped out. He called me all kinds of whores. But it was all good especially since Muscle Man was on duty that day. He drug him out of there like he was carrying an infant."

"I bet that's the same dude that was there the day we went. He wanted to get him then." Jamal was acting as if he was excitedly cheering for his favorite team.

Jamal just fell out on the floor laughing; free. Divine knew that this conversation was going to work out for the good. She's the kind of mother that would do anything for her children including being strong enough to teach them firsthand the power of forgiving your enemy.

# CHAPTER 33

C hristian was now walking with just a cane. His determination had catapulted his healing. Although walking on a cane made him feel like an old man it was a whole lot better than with the crutches. He could see the progress that he was making.

At this point he had altogether given up on asking Kerry questions about his past since she was so vague with her answers. He needed details and names. But the only thing she thought about was herself. She had even been pressuring him to marry her. Had it been before all the doubts that had come up, he probably would have complied. For now he used his amnesia as a stalling point for he had no idea who he was engaged to or what she was truly capable of.

As the three of them rode into civilization he looked around taking in the sights that he had only seen a few times before. He was happy to ride with her and his son to the doctor especially today since he had a plan.

He noticed a library not far from the doctor's office the last time that they came. Christian was determined to find some answers. There was new information that was burning his brain that he had to research.

After getting into the doctor's office and signing in, Christian made an excuse that would get him outside where he planned to go onto his big excursion.

"I got such a bad headache. I'm going to go outside to get some fresh air."

Kerry looked up momentarily from her magazine to smile at him.

"Ok sweetie," she said in such a perky voice that it almost gave him a real headache.

Once outside, Christian's stride picked up. His cane and step had a rhythm. By the time that he got up the steps to the library, his heart rate was definitely up. He walked through the doors looking around to see a young lady that was just enough outside of her teens to be out of high school.

Her look didn't match the small town that she was in. She had blonde hair which was her normal color but the chunks of extreme black most definitely had to be dye. There was something about the eye ring that screamed that she was trying to rebel against the boredom of her immediate society. The look in her eyes seemed friendly. He approached the desk that she sat behind.

"Hey there," Christian said.

"Hey. How are you doing?" she replied back in a friendly tone.

"I'm good but could be doing better." He smiled lifting his cane.

She let out a little giggle of understanding before Christian continued on.

"I need some help. I have total amnesia and I want to find some information on myself."

"Whoa! Really?" The young lady was shocked. She had never been face-to-face with someone that had that condition before. Christian wasn't offended. With the size of the town that is what he expected.

"Yep. So I need some help."

"Alrighty. You came to the right one. I can find anyone on the internet plus a little dirt and gossip." She nodded her head with high confidence in her skills.

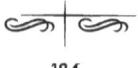

SON OF THE FORGIVEN

"Great." Christian laughed at her display. On the inside he rejoiced that he was going to find some answers.

"So Sir, do you mind me asking how your memory got wiped out?"

"No. Not at all. I was in a car accident and stayed in a coma for almost a year. I just woke up a couple of months ago."

"Hope you don't think that I was being nosy. Just curious." She smiled before continuing. "So what's your name?"

"Christian David Jackson."

"And where did you live?"

"Well, I woke up in Alabama but the accident occurred in New York."

"How did someone in a coma make that journey?"

"That's what I'm trying to figure out," Christian replied.

"Got something! A newspaper article. You were in a car accident in New York where the car left the road and the female driver, Julia Vile, didn't survive the accident but you did and you were in critical condition and in a coma."

"Julia Vile. Mmm. So that's her name. Well that wasn't the name that I remember." Christian turned the name over in his head to see if anything else would come about her. The only thing he remembered was the actual accident right as it was happening.

"Did that help any?" She raised the eyebrow which lifted the ring that was pierced in it.

"Some. It put a name to a face in my memory. I remembered another name but just the first and I was wondering if you could search that with my name."

"Sure. What is it?"

"Kenali."

185

She took the name and began to click swiftly on the keyboard. Then she clicked the mouse a couple of times.

"Congratulations to you! She's beautiful," She exclaimed as if she was talking to someone that she had known for a while. Christian was totally clueless.

"What are you talking about?" His thought became verbal.

"You're engaged." The young researcher had delivered on her promise for this was something that he wished that he could gossip about. She turned the computer monitor around so that he could see the picture of the both of them holding each other smiling.

"It's her," Christian whispered very lowly. He almost wanted to pass out. He was so confused that he had to struggle to stand. How could he be engaged to Kenali *also*?

"The rest of the write up kind of explain how you got to Alabama. She's a writer that lives in Alabama and you're in advertisement in New York. OMG! I've read some of her books." The young researcher came to excited awareness. She couldn't believe that she was face-to-face with the fiancé of a writer that she was familiar with.

Christian was so dazed at this point. His helper was going on and on while his head was swirling as fast as her mouth was going.

"What's her last name?" Christian couldn't think.

"King. Her name is Kenali King. And here's one of her books. It's my own personal book so you can have it. Are you ok?"

Christian reached out for the book that had her smiling photo on the back cover. He was still so floored. With his fingertips he traced the lines of her face wondering how they got separated like this.

Before he could get himself together, his cell phone began to ring. It was his so called fiancée Kerry. He took in a deep breath before he talked to her since he never wanted her to know what he just learned. Not until he had the whole puzzle together.

"I'll be right there. I just took a little walk."

He hung up the phone. Before he walked out, he thanked the young lady that had so greatly helped him. He didn't know when but he was definitely coming back to find the rest of the answers.

One thing that he knew was that Kenali apparently was looking for him since she and the police was at the last place that he lived. His mind churned over this mystery as he limped back to the car to ride with someone that is now considered the enemy. Mentally he started a countdown to the end of their time together.

# CHAPTER 34

Christian lay there beside this imposter, looking at her while she slept unaware that he knew that she was up to something. He still could not figure out what role she played in his life or the motivation behind it. There was something strange that he couldn't put his finger on. But the same was true for most of his memory.

After all, he didn't want to jump to conclusions. There was a wide gap in his memory that a lot could have transpired between the three of them. Surely he wasn't a player that was just going around having women fall in love with him only stringing them along with the hope of being Mrs. Jackson. Even though he couldn't remember, that just didn't feel like the kind of person he was despite the fact that he was somehow stuck in the middle of a web of three females and a baby.

Since the day at the library, he had barely slept. He told himself that he had to keep an eye on this lady until some clarity came. Christian was at the point that he rather owe her an apology than put all of his trust in her. He didn't know how but he was going to get to the bottom of this and soon. He needed to get to the library again.

Christian eased out of the bed to sneak off to the bathroom. He quietly locked the door behind him. Then removing the lid off the toilet tank, he reached inside to get the book that the girl had given him. He took it out of the Ziploc bag that kept it from getting wet.

Every night he had the same routine. He would flip it to the back cover to look at Kenali's photo before he would read the words from the pages. Although he couldn't remember, he knew that he loved her even when she didn't have a name other than beautiful woman from his dreams.

His actions almost made him feel like he was sneaking drugs or something. But he was addicted to the book therefore he took it everywhere with him. He would sit by the water wondering if he was the man that she was talking about in this novel. The description fit him to a "T".

Christian became saddened to know that there was only a few more pages before he was finished reading about the love that they shared that stood up through every tribulation. The more that he read, the more real that she became to him. He could see her personality through her words.

"I will find you," he whispered to himself while looking at the picture. He was making a decree that he was going to find out whatever he needed to know so that he could make the appropriate decisions.

Then his mind clicked. He was going back to the old apartment in the morning. He was pretty sure that he was going to dig up something there amidst all that dirt.

So for the next couple of hours, he placed the work that was written by his real fiancée back into the tank. He needed just a little sleep so that he would have enough energy to venture out. Before long, just like in the pages of the novel, they would be together happily.

---

Christian must have slept a lot heavier than he thought. He woke up to the aroma of breakfast. He could hear her humming in the kitchen along with the rattle of the dishes. If

she was the real one for him, he could get use to her but he had something for Kenali that he couldn't explain; a strong love that was pulling him.

Christian got up, which that was getting easier as the days went by. While getting dressed, he planned things out in his head. He knew that he couldn't stray too far off his regular routine as he didn't want to alert her of anything.

He strolled into the kitchen wearing sweats and sneakers as he did daily for his workout that he had designed.

"Good morning," Christian said trying to sound as normal as possible.

"Good morning. Did you sleep well?" She sounded very chipper and well rested. It must be the fact that she is sleeping with someone that has amnesia he thought.

"I slept ok." *Could've slept better if I knew the truth,* Christian thought.

"Breakfast is almost ready."

"Ok," Christian replied looking at the back of her head wishing that he could know what was going on inside of it. He started to say that he wasn't going to wait but that would have been too different. So he patiently looked out the window going over the plan in his head.

Walk to the main road, thumb a ride, go to the apartment complex, catch a ride to the library and then back here before I'm missed. Well planned. Christian didn't see any reason why it wouldn't be successful.

A plate being sat down in front of him broke his attention.

"Thank you," he instinctively said.

"You're welcome," she replied. "So do you have any plans after you finish training?"

Christian thought for a moment. Why would she ask him that when she never did? Had he somehow let on that he knew something? He had to answer according to his usual routine.

"No. Just watch a little t.v. and play with Jr. Why?"

"I was just wondering if you wanted to go to a nearby city which is much larger than here. Since you're walking so well I thought that maybe you would like to take Jr. for a stroll through a real park. Then the three of us could have a picnic. Wouldn't that be great?"

"Yes, that would be great. Just let me get a little rest after my workout and I'll be ready to go." Christian was still more excited about his newly planned workout for the day than the opportunity to get away from these trees. He couldn't wait. Depending on what information he got would determine if Jr. and he would be strolling through any park with her.

He shoveled his food into his mouth like a savage that hadn't eaten in a long time. Christian was being pulled by finding the truth.

He went into the bathroom to retrieve the book hidden there. He rested it between the waistband of his briefs and his skin. Pulling his sweatshirt over it, he checked in the mirror to see if it was noticeable. It wasn't.

When he strolled into the kitchen, he kissed her on the forehead then picked up his son from her arms to kiss him also. Since he mentioned it, she had been holding him more. Actually she had been acting a whole lot better since the day that she burned her hand. His thoughts were that she knew that he was on to her. That's why he forfeited on asking anymore questions to see if she would make any more mistakes.

Christian returned his son back to his original cradle in Kerry's arms. Then he picked up his cell phone from the charger which proved to be mistake number one.

"Why are you getting your cell phone? You know there isn't any service out here."

Christian got deathly still. He continued to hold the cord of the charger. He needed to think fast.

"I need it to keep track of time since I'm not wearing a watch. I might cut my workout short today since I'll be going on a picnic with my wonderful fiancée and my great son. What more could a man ask for?" He lied his way out of suspicion. He needed the cell phone for his independent outing that was planned for the day.

"Be careful honey." Without a clue of anything being outside of what he said, she smiled at him.

"Alright. See you in a little while." He touched her shoulder and she placed her hand on top of his. He tried to do everything that he normally did before he had this truth.

The road was a half mile hike through trees that was full of brush, fallen branches, and other debris which would make it a hard journey. The other day he stumbled upon a trail that hadn't been attended to recently but it was far better than the other alternative. It would make his travel faster.

He focused on the time knowing that he had to hurry. Christian picked up the crutches that he had hidden out here the other day for the purpose that he would be able to travel faster with them. They would allow him to swing through the air flying over a lot of things that he would have to be careful to walk on.

His pace was steadily fueled by determination. The idea came from watching the Animal Channel when he saw a gorilla that was cutting his way through the jungle on his extended arms. Now Christian used these crutches like the arms of the gorilla to get out of this jungle.

Finally he had arrived at the road where he placed the crutches down removing his cane that had been strapped to one of them. As he limped down this dirt road that led to the main highway, he hoped that someone would be passing by to give him a ride. Even greater, he hoped that someone would be quicker to pick him up since he was on a cane.

When he made it to the paved road an 18-wheeler had just passed by causing his sweats to flap in the wind. Then he removed the book from inside his waistband. It was stuck to his skin from his perspiration. He wiped it onto his pant leg. Situating himself, he began to stride toward the direction of town.

It wasn't long before a nice old man stopped on an equally old pickup truck that had some hogs on the back that were squealing and grunting loudly.

"Where ya headed?" He yelled over the combination of noises from pigs and a pickup that sputtered.

"I'm going into town. To the library." Christian held up the book that he had just recently and conveniently revealed. It would have been awkward pulling it out of his shorts in front of this man to ask for a ride.

"Hop on in. I'm going right by there."

"Thanks." Christian grabbed the handle pushing the button to release the latch. Climbing in, he sat upon old leather seats that had been ripped exposing its innards of mustard yellow foam.

The old man looked at the cane that Christian placed by his left leg before slamming the door shut.

"You mighty young to be on a cane. What happened?" The old man looked in the direction of his cane before looking at Christian.

"I was in a car accident about a year ago. I don't plan to be on this cane much longer but it is helpful right now."

"That's how it is sometimes. You have to use things to help you up and then release it when it's time. That's true for people too." The old man looked over at Christian nodding his head.

Christian understood what he was saying all too well. He was in that exact type of dilemma now where he felt like it was time to release someone from his life. Previously he had felt kind of guilty about wanting to be away from her but with everything unfolding the way it has been plus with how this old man who knew nothing of his situation gave him the right wise words, there was no way that he could continue to feel convicted.

The two men continue to ride down the highway with the windows down letting in the cool breezes of the fall air. Their conversation covered pig farming, relationships, children and grandchildren, and all sorts of things. Christian even found out that the place that he is living now is called the old Gipson cabin which had a lot of history swarming it.

Had it been more interesting than his own history he would have looked it up when he entered the library. After thanking the old man, he all but ran up the steps. This time when he entered the library, the young investigator that was there the other day wasn't there. She had been replaced by an elderly lady that wore her glasses on the tip of her nose with a metal beaded chain holding them in case they fell. He hoped that she could help him also.

"Good morning." Her voice rang out holding onto every word as if to extend the greeting to give him time to reach the desk where she sat.

"Good morning," Christian returned the greeting.

"What could I do for you today?" She asked.

"I came in a few days ago and a young lady helped me with a search on the internet. I wanted to come in to search some more."

The lady drew up like she had sucked a lemon.

"All this modern technology. I don't even know how to use the computer. I like to stick to the old way of using the card catalog. I've been a librarian for over 40 years and I betcha I'm faster than any computer."

Christian was discouraged but he wasn't going to give up that easy.

"Do you mind if I use your computer?"

"Well we aren't supposed to let anybody use them plus I don't know the password to get on the darn thing. What are you looking for? I told you I can help you find it in the catalog." This older lady was convinced that she could be of help. It would have wrecked her ego to know that her way of doing things was like seeing a dinosaur today.

"What I'm looking for wouldn't be in the card catalog. It's stuff that has just happened." Christian put his hand on his side to think.

She had to recognize that the card catalog wouldn't have that. "Oh I'm so sorry, Honey."

"Oh. It's ok. When will the other girl be back?"

"Christmas break. She's in college and we're so proud of her."

Now he was crushed. There was no way that he was going to wait all that time before he found out what was going on in his life. Hopefully by Christmas he was going to be with the right woman shopping for gifts for her and his son.

Christian thanked the woman just out of pure habit. He wasn't completely crushed since he did have one more stop to make. Hopefully going to the apartment would be more fruitful than this. It was just a few short blocks away. Christian walked with the thoughts that it wouldn't be as disappointing as the library.

Arriving there, he saw the kid that he had befriended the brief time that he stayed there. He was sitting outside doing the same thing that he was doing the first time he saw him; playing a handheld video game. If you didn't know any better you would think that he was a lot younger than what he actually was. He was fourteen but looked to be no older than ten.

When he looked up from his game to see Christian, his feet started moving before they hit the floor.

"Dude! You're in so much trouble. Everybody has been looking for you." The kid's mouth was going a mile a minute. Christian had to slow him down.

"Whoa. Whoa. Whoa. Now what are you talking about? Start at the beginning and go slow." Christian's heart naturally started beating to the sound of confirmation that this visit was going to be productive.

"The last day you were here, the cops came by looking for the baby that had been kidnapped."

"What baby?"

"Yo baby, dude." The kid bucked his eyes at Christian as if he was saying "duh".

"How's my baby considered kidnapped?" Christian couldn't understand.

"Because it's yo baby and her baby but the her is not the one that's with you but the lady from Bama is the mama. And she came to get her baby but y'all didn't show back up no more. Bama went slap off on the po po. You should have seen it. That chic got fire." This kid was so happy to be reporting this news to Christian. He excitedly waved his hands with every other word.

Christian's mind was churning trying to decipher what he just heard. Then Kenali popped into his mind.

"Are you talking about Kenali King?"

"Yep. That's Bama's name."

"Do you know how to get into contact with her?"

"I can e-mail her. She's all over the internet looking for her baby. Everybody knows about David. He's a famous lil dude."

Christian thought for a moment and left instructions to his teenaged friend. He had to rush back to the house to protect his son. He now knew why Kerry said, "*your son*".

# CHAPTER 35

K enali paced back and forth in front of her desk. She wanted so desperately to hear a chime from someone that had some answers to the whereabouts of her son. The more time that she and David were apart the more anxious that she felt. She was anxious to hold him again and all the other motherly things that she had done for him.

She had been so close to having him back that to give up now was ridiculous. Kenali knew that this time when she got a nugget she was going to be on it like a hot potato. There would be no phone call to Detective Morris. If she had followed her gut instinct the last time then she probably would have had her son back.

The trip wasn't a total waste since she did find out from the kid that sent in the picture that Christian had told him that he had total amnesia. Momentarily she had given up hope that they would ever be together again. But God. God decided to give her a ray of sunshine to let her know to hold on to the love that was in her heart towards Christian.

Yet she paced the floor cracking her knuckles with every other step. Her body lunged at the computer when she heard the chime which was music to her ears. After reading the message, replying a big thank you, she grabbed her keys. Off to Arkansas she was going again. This time she wasn't coming back empty handed. She was coming back with her son and her man.

On the way, she played over how she would act when she held David again. Then her mind further ventured to how she would feel to see Christian awake even though he would only vaguely know who she was. Thanks to her teenage informant, she knew that he was at least looking for her now. And it was great to know that their son was safe with him.

She had so many people to thank. There was Jamal for his unending plastering of the missing trio on the internet. If it weren't for him, she didn't know what she would have done. Then there was Lane & Simbol who found out about Christian and this woman. Kenali felt like she was going to be on an awards show having to prep a speech about who she was going to thank so that she wouldn't offend anybody by absentmindedly leaving their name off.

So many thoughts were going through her head of what she was going to do in just a few short hours when she arrived. Although she was still angry with the police force in Skippleton, she was going to call them one more time but only after she got her hands on this woman's neck for stealing her baby. This chick was going to jail but not before she got a beat down.

Before she could turn this whooping over in her head enough to bring her satisfaction, her phone rang. It was Jamal.

"Why did you leave me?"

"How did you know that I was gone?"

"I got a CC of the e-mail."

Technology was a teenager's pastime. They knew every angle of it therefore there is no way that she could ever sneak anything past him.

"I felt like it was going to be too dangerous for you to go this round plus you need to spend some time with your mom and dad. They need you right now."

"They alright. You need me to be your backup. I could've held lil cuz while you went ham on ol' girl."

"Child, get out of my head. That's what I was just thinking." Kenali was glad that he did know. She never liked to leave town without someone knowing where she was. Realistically she didn't want anything to happen to Jamal while she was chasing after her son.

"That's cause I know you Special K. How far have you gotten?"

"I'm 2 hours up the road."

"Dang, aunt Kenali. I don't want you to go by yourself. We're going to be right behind you."

"Who is we?" Kenali could tell that by the way Jamal was talking that he was serious. In fact, she wouldn't be surprised if they were already riding now.

"Me, mama, daddy, aunt Simbol and uncle Lane. We in the Tahoe an hour behind you. We would have been closer but yo' sister Simbol is so slow."

Kenali could hear Simbol in the background with her rebuttal. Then there was interjection from everyone to agree with Jamal.

Kenali knew that Jamal had put that together. He was always able to get the family to move when he had his mind set on something. She was thankful to have the help. Strength came to her as she really put the pedal to the metal now knowing that her family had her back; literally.

# CHAPTER 36

C hristian finally got back to the cabin with his heart beating so fast that it felt as if it would leap from his chest. It wasn't beating like that because of how fast he was moving but to know that his son was in the hands of an abductor.

Who was Kerry he thought when he saw her through the window holding his son as he hurriedly climbed the steps? He tried to calm himself since he didn't know the magnitude of what she was capable of. At the doorway, he held onto the knob and prayed before entering.

"Lord, I confessed that you're my Lord and Savior. I need you to save me and my son now."

Christian walked through the door walking straight towards her. He had to get his child into his arms.

"You look like you had a very hard workout," Kerry said completely unaware of Christian's knowledge.

Reaching for his son, she pulled away from him.

"You're all sweaty and he's already dressed to go on the picnic."

Briefly Christian knew what Kenali felt having her baby taken from her. He was too close to fail.

"I'll change him. I just need to hold him. It's a guy thing. You wouldn't understand."

"I'm going to hold you to changing him cause our son is so fidgety when he is getting his clothes put on." Kerry sounded so happy.

He almost gagged trying to hold in the words that he wanted to yell at her.

"It's no problem. Daddy's home and he don't do all that with daddy."

Christian held his son tightly, kissing him on the forehead, absorbing his baby scent. He did everything that he could to keep from reaching over to knock this woman out. It just didn't feel right to hit a woman but this one deserved it. Calming himself, he had to think now of his son's safety.

He stalled for as long as he could before he had to go shower and get dressed. He couldn't hold her off any longer. The last thing on his mind was going on a picnic with her but that would place him in a public area that should the strength of his legs fail him he could probably get some help from a passerby. She wouldn't harm a baby in public—he hoped not.

# CHAPTER 37

This time Kenali barely needed the GPS to show her the way. When she pulled up to the apartment complex, she hurriedly ran to the apartment that her teenage helper stayed in. He identified himself in the e-mail as Markus. Knocking on the door, she wondered which of his parents would open it but to her surprise it was him.

"Hey, Ms. King," he boyishly greeted her as if she was his favorite school teacher.

"Hey, Markus. Thank you so much for helping me."

"You're welcome." Markus shyly smiled before continuing. "He left the address they're living at now but it won't show up on GPS so I have to take you."

"Is that ok with your parents?" Kenali tried to look around him but didn't notice anyone inside of the front room. The room was dark for the time of day but the light from the television flickered.

"Yeah. They don't mind. They're at work anyway."

At any rate, Kenali knew that she wouldn't bring any harm to him especially since he was helping her to find David.

She travelled swiftly turning where Markus instructed her to. He knew these back roads like the back of his own hand.

She called to notify her family that she was on her way out to the cabin and where it was located. Then before she could finish her last sentence, the cell service faded.

"That's the invisible line that cell phone service don't cross which is the reason that he told me to text him." Markus filled her in so that she wouldn't waste an attempt to call her family back.

"Oh," Kenali said as she turned onto a dirt road that was darkened almost as if nighttime had come only to this area. The density of the trees blocked out all light as they hung over the road. After travelling the bumpy road for what seemed like miles, she then saw the tire tracks across grass that had to be a driveway. She followed them finally up to a cabin.

There wasn't a car parked where the tracks ended. Kenali decided to get out. When she opened her door, Markus, her little navigator did the same.

"Stay here," she instructed him as she had no idea what she was walking into.

She walked up the old wooden steps slowly hoping that it wouldn't break. Then on the porch she looked inside the front door window. She didn't notice any movement anywhere. She knocked anyway.

After there wasn't any response she walked around the porch that wrapped around three sides of the cabin. When she got to the bedroom, she could see a crib by the window with a little baby blue blanket that looked like it had been pulled back from her son when he was picked up. Tears began to form in her eyes. She was so close to getting her baby back that these tears felt like victory.

Since nothing or no one was there, she walked back to join her new friend who was eagerly waiting to know what she came across.

"Whatcha find?" Markus inquisitively questioned.

"Nothing but I do see a crib and some clothing lying around. It looks like they must have left not too long ago."

"So what are we gonna do now?" Markus was intending on riding this out to the end. He reminded Kenali of Jamal.

"We're going to go back into town to see what else we can find. Maybe they went to a store. Do you know what kind of car they drive?"

"Sure do." He was excited to be of some help to Kenali.

As they rode along, they crossed back over the invisible line. Shortly after, both of their phones began chirping from missed messages.

Kenali's message was from her family wondering what happened. Markus' message was a text from Christian telling him where this family of three was going.

"Christian is headed to Stanton to a park."

"What?" Kenali exclaimed with disbelief. She partly felt it strange that they would be gallivanting around with a kidnapped baby. Yet it was good that they would be in public.

"He sent me a text. He sent it about thirty minutes ago. So they should be getting there soon. It's a forty-five minute drive."

"I passed through there on my way. My family is probably passing through there right now."

Kenali quickly dialed Jamal's phone number. When he answered, he started talking but Kenali had to shush him.

"Jamal, where are you all right now?"

"Hold on." He took the phone away from his face but she heard him ask his dad their whereabouts.

Gerald responded loud enough for Kenali to hear it over the speaker. "We're passing through a place called Stanton."

"You gotta stop there. Christian is headed that way to go to a park," Kenali rushed her words out.

Jamal didn't waste any time getting the message out.

"Pull over! Christian is headed this way," He yelled with much excitement.

While he was filling everyone in on what was going on, Kenali handed the phone to her quest mate.

"Can you describe what kind of car they are on to him so they can look out for it?"

Markus began talking to Jamal while Kenali sped back over the road in which she had come. She decided that her new partner was a valuable asset to her therefore she would keep him. While she drove, Kenali prayed that this doesn't turn out like the last time.

# CHAPTER 38

"What is that buzzing noise that I keep hearing?" Kerry looked at Christian through the rearview mirror. He was sitting in the backseat with his son as she drove.

"I'm just messing around with an alarm that I found on the phone today. I figured that it could be some help to me when I workout." Christian had already premeditated that lie when he heard it buzz from receiving the first text message. Kerry was very sharp and noticed everything. He guessed that was what came with the package of being a kidnapper.

"Oh ok." The answer seemed to satisfy Kerry somewhat although her eyesight still lingered in the mirror. Christian's head was still down as he was engulfed in what he was doing.

Now since she was asking questions, Christian decided to ask a few of his own.

"Who were our friends?" He looked up into the rearview mirror getting eye contact with her. He noticed that same fidgety look whenever he asked her something about their past.

"Well they were slim. I worked long shifts being a nurse and you were a loner. You just kind of kept to yourself," Kerry sounded only slightly convincing to him.

If he hadn't doubted their past together he probably would have believed her. So he decided to ask more direct questions based on the information that he had found out recently.

"Oh that's why where we live doesn't bother me. So what kind of job did I have?"

Kerry paused awkwardly. "You know that I shouldn't be telling you all of this. Remember it's best that you get your memory back on your own from mental cues like the place that we're going now. I'm hoping that it helps you to remember."

Once again a vague answer that didn't answer anything. But he wasn't letting go this time.

"How would Stanton be a mental cue for me? Have we been here before?"

"No not so much the city but the park. I hate that you don't remember one of our most important days." Kerry was trying to sound saddened by some memory that neither one of them had or would ever have.

Christian was very dry. "And what day is that?" His coldness dried up any fictitious intent that she was trying to pullover on him.

"The day we got engaged. You don't remember anything about that time?" Kerry tried to sound so solemn that it sickened Christian. He thought on the tricks that he had up his sleeve that he would display as soon as they walked through the park.

"Maybe it'll be best if I wait until we get to the park like you said. I really do want to remember."

Christian did remember the day that he got engaged. He remembered the kneeling down onto one knee standing in front of a river looking up into the face of Kenali King asking her to marry him. That memory came in a dream some time ago but he didn't understand it until he saw the engagement announcement at the library.

Yes indeed. Kerry was in for the shock of her life. He had confirmation that his teenaged buddy Markus had really pulled through for him. The truth was definitely going to come out realistically today.

They arrived at the park shortly after they finished their conversation. He really didn't feel like much talking. Not to her anyway. Once getting out of the car, he hopped around to the trunk to get the baby stroller out. There were a lot of things that a baby needed that had to be carried. He felt like half the stuff that was being hauled around was for just in case.

While putting Jr. in the stroller, Christian loaded the baby bag underneath. He pulled the cover over his stroller so that the sun wouldn't be in his face.

"You look tired," Kerry commented.

"Really? I don't feel tired. Actually I feel pretty good right about now." Christian was telling the truth. He knew that it wasn't going to be much longer before all the charades were over. Knowing the real story behind who Kerry really was sat on the top of the list.

"Good. Then let's venture into this park to have a great time," she perkily replied.

Kerry pushed the stroller across the street while Christian carried the picnic basket in one hand using the cane in the other. Had it not been for the timed crosswalk, he didn't know if he could have made it in enough time. This was a busy street and sprinting hadn't come completely to him without the use of his crutches.

"Oh my God that's Christian!" Divine shouted out.

"Where?" Every eye in the Tahoe was searching diligently for him.

"Up there, going across the street!" Simbol responded when she locked eyes on him also.

"Wow. What do we do?" Divine asked out of total confusion. She wanted to jump out to run them down to grab her nephew but was afraid that she would alarm Kerry to make her do something drastic.

"Ok. We're going to park the car. All of us need to be on the ground at different angles so that she can't get away," Lane voiced his opinion. It was logical therefore everyone was in agreement.

"Jamal, get your auntie on the phone and let her know we have a visual," Gerald said with a military tone.

"Eye, eye captain." Jamal followed the orders.

Gerald pulled over into the parking lot. Everybody jumped out as fast as they could including Jamal.

"Stay here, son," Gerald firmly spoke.

"But dad," Jamal brokenheartedly whined. He wanted a piece of the action since he had come so far with this.

"Look, son. I don't know anything about that woman or what frame of mind Christian is in. Keeping you safe is priority number one. So I need you to stay here. That's a car that fit the description that the kid gave you. If you see her come back to that car to leave, you lay on this horn. Ok." Gerald placed his hand on the side of Jamal's face.

Jamal let out a sigh letting everyone know that he was not happy at all about the decision. He obediently watched them cross the street to enter the park.

A few minutes later, Jamal saw Kenali pull in on two wheels. He jumped out and pointed in the direction that they went. She instructed Markus to stay with Jamal. Then she ran swiftly across the street. Once inside she spotted Lane, who was standing by a tree looking.

"Where are they?" Kenali asked.

"Over there. We have them surrounded at every angle." Lane was filling her in on what was going on but she stopped listening after the most sought after trio entered her eyesight.

Kenali was headed straight for them boldly. She was getting her baby back today. Christian had his back to her but Kerry spotted Kenali immediately. She knew she was in for it so she took flight. Kerry took off running with the stroller so fast that Christian barely had time to know what was going on.

He spun around to see Kenali sprinting after this woman with other people coming from other angles. He limped as fast as he could after his son wishing that he had the crutches. Desperation jumped into his broken but healed bones.

Kerry was running toward a music festival screaming as loud as she could.

"Help, there trying to get my baby."

A helpful mob of people detained all of them except Kenali although going through the crowd did slow her down. There was a growing gap between her and her baby yet she was determined that today was the day that she held David again.

Kenali could no longer see them since Kerry had turned the curve. Kenali's adrenaline kicked in as she pushed her sprint into top gear. Christian spotted her going around the trees taking off behind her. He winced at the pain that jolted through his body. Yet he pushed on becoming less aware of the pain. His son was in the hands of the wrong person.

By this time, the others had explained that Kerry was the kidnapper. Divine conveniently had the missing person's flyer in her hand which had Kerry's photo plastered as the abductor. Now this mob was all seeking Kerry.

The farther that Gerald and the others got away from the music, they could hear the faint sound of the horn. They knew that Jamal had spotted Kerry. They ran to the entrance which was so far away.

Before Kerry could get completely to the crosswalk, Kenali reached out to her grabbing the only thing that she could; a hand full of hair. Kerry turned around to swing on her. Kenali ducked.

The two ladies got into an all-out tussle exchanging words as they struggled.

"You crazy heifer, you messed up when you stole my baby."

"Let go of me! I'm not crazy," Kerry said through gritted teeth. She was angry that she was being detained.

Kerry saw Christian coming as well as a mob of people. She needed a way out fast. She managed to slip from Kenali's grip and swung on her once more. She missed again.

"Since you're so good at ducking, can you dodge?"

As soon as she said it, Kerry turned with all of her force and pushed the stroller into the busy street with oncoming traffic. Tires started screeching. With everything that said that she was the true mother of that baby, Kenali ran fiercely into the street to push her baby out of harm's way but it was not the same for her.

Christian ran to grab their son out of the stroller.

Divine cried out as she ran to the street followed by the others, "Somebody call an ambulance!"

"Kenali, I'm sorry I didn't know you. I could only remember how much I loved you." With his mind full of tears; Christian's eyes did likewise.

Gasping vigorously with blood filling her mouth, she could only think of one thing. "Where's my son?"

"Our son is right here. You saved him just like a good mother would."

"I need to see him." Granting her wish, Christian put David in front of his mother's eyes. Through all of her pain, she managed to smile and leave final words with the one little man that never disappointed her. "I love you, son of my forgiven sin."

# CHAPTER 39

"**W**hy did you kidnap the baby?" Detective Morris continued to interrogate Kerry.

"I didn't. He's my baby. I took care of him. He's mine." Kerry was excruciatingly trying to convince them of the reality that was only in her own head. Tears poured from her eyes while snot ran from her nose.

Assuming that to be the only answer that he would get from her on that question, Detective Morris decided to go onto other questions.

"How did you know Christian Jackson?"

Halfheartedly, he expected an answer on his side of sanity. He looked at Kerry sternly as she rocked back and forth with her hands clasped together in the center of her chest.

When the question reached the center of her brain, she stilled herself. Staring off into the distance, she answered. "I knew him in the midst of rejection. He was the reason that she didn't notice me anymore."

"She? Who are you talking about?" Detective Morris inquired.

Kerry continued as if he had never said anything.

"It was something about him that she just had to have. I told her that he would only hurt her, make her life miserable.

Every time I thought that she needed me, she only wanted me to listen to how Kenali was getting *her man*." Kerry paused. Continually she rubbed her hands and scratched her head. Then she swallowed hard before going on.

"At first, I prayed that Kenali would get him once and for all. Then she and I could go back to being what we were before Christian showed up. I was always there. There being stepped on. There being rejected because he was in the picture now."

Then Kerry looked farther off into the distance as if that memory was playing live video on the wall that was just blank to everyone else. Lane wished so greatly that she could answer the question of who was this person that had wrecked the lives of them all because she rejected Kerry. Although he thought that he knew, he continued to allow his patience to be tried. Annoyed, Lane looked at Detective Morris wondering if he could shake a straight answer out of her. He wanted her to get straight to the point but he realized that he wasn't dealing with the usual person therefore he elected to wait it out.

Then Kerry's stare was broken as she looked at him holding her head sideways not knowing whether to trust him or not.

"You know things changed after the accident. I saw them bring him into the hospital all broken up and bloody. I almost lost it when they said that there was another victim, a female, that didn't survive. I knew that it was her."

Now Lane was putting the pieces together of who this woman was that Kerry was talking about. It was all coming to light now.

Kerry creepily continued. "The whole time that she was in the morgue, I would go down to comb her hair and tell her that things would get better when she just gave up the idea that she and Christian would be together. Then Kenali came to take care of Christian which made me know that I was doing the right thing. People take care of people that they love. So I had to take care of her."

Now Kerry's look changed to something twisted as if someone had secretly whispered something evil into her ear.

"Then they came to put her in the ground where I could no longer take care of her. Then Christian was taken away by Kenali but she at least still had him. I planned to settle the score with him for what he had done to her. You understand, right?"

Lane just looked at her in silence. He could not believe what he was hearing. He was almost frightened to speak since he didn't want to set her off in any kind of way. He wanted to throw up.

Detective Morris sensed this deciding to once again ask for a name. And once again, his question went unnoticed.

"So who is this woman that you are talking about, Kerry?"

She looked at Lane completely ignoring Detective Morris. "I knew you would understand. We have a lot in common. I can tell. You love your wife a lot and wouldn't want anybody to hurt her would you?"

Lane knew that she was now asking the questions leaving him to wonder who had the upper hand. Yet it was something on the inside that wanted her to keep going so he could get to the why part of her actions. Lane looked at Detective Morris before answering who nodded giving him the go ahead.

"No, I wouldn't," Lane answered dryly since he didn't want to anyway.

"And that was the same way that I felt about her. Christian hurt her. Kenali hurt her. That's why they had to hurt. Keeping them love birds apart hurt them a lot. See how smart I am." Kerry abruptly stopped talking.

Lane had his answer. He had stomached enough of this. Therefore he decided to take the enemy out with one blow.

"That chick's name was Julia but you can't say it. Normal people don't go around acting like the two of you. But you're right about one thing; she should have placed it in her twisted lil brain that Christian didn't want her. I told Christian that she's going to be trouble. I just didn't know that it was going to be from the grave too."

Lane got up looking her square in the eyes to see how the look inside them stayed the same while her facial expression changed drastically with her every phrase. As he walked away, she said something that made him stay.

"I'll tell you everything but only to you." She was pointing at Lane with her head down. Kerry's demeanor looked like something out of a horror movie.

Detective Morris intervened. "Look you need to say what you gotta say and now."

"You can leave the room. I'm good." Lane really wanted to know what she had to say that was so important that only he could hear it.

Detective Morris looked at Lane who shook his head that it was alright.

"You have five minutes." Detective Morris looked at Kerry firmly letting her know that he meant business and was tired of her games.

After Detective Morris exited the room, Lane sat down across from Kerry.

"So whatcha gotta tell me?" Lane was clearly irritated.

Kerry looked him straight in the eye with full sanity. Whispering, she began to speak.

"Look Trick, I'm neither a lesbian nor crazy. Insanity is just a good cop out. I'll be out shortly since Kenali didn't die and Stanton PD didn't read me my rights. So although my plan got messed up, it's still all good. I was going to keep moving Christian and his son so that Kenali would never find them. Why? Because he hurt Julia more than anyone will ever know."

"So all of this is because Christian broke up with Julia? Get over it!" Lane was aggravated.

"Shut up! I didn't ask you to speak. As I was saying, when he rejected her to go back to Kenali, Julia slid back into her drug addiction. And guess where she picked that habit up from? You. Julia got addicted to drugs on the streets of Alabama by your low down drug dealing hands. All of this was to get to you. Your cousin got it easy. Now had my plan worked I would have been in here for the murder of you and your blushing bride since the two of you were so hot and heavy on my trail." Kerry was infuriated but aware of the height of her voice.

Lane looked shocked. His past that he was forgiven for still had repercussions. Sinking into his brain was the threat that she just made against Simbol. It angered him.

"You better stay away from my family! You are sick. I don't live that life no more. I'm forgiven." From Lane's shouting, Kerry knew that she had hit a nerve.

Then she continued to whisper harshly through clenched teeth. Although there wasn't any windows in this room that Detective Morris could be watching her from behind, Kerry still didn't want what she was saying to be heard.

"Be sure to tell your family that all of this is your fault and see how forgiven you are by them. I'll never forgive you. Look for me in a few years, Trick. Vengeance is mine!"

Kerry put a smirk on her face, winking her eye at an irate Lane.

Lane went ballistic flipping the table that sat between him and Kerry. Before Lane could get his hands on her, Detective Morris burst through the door to restrain him.

Conveniently, Kerry reverted back to her insanity charades.

"I can say her name. I love Julia. How do you know her name? I love Julia for life. Give me my baby back."

Vengeance had now imprisoned Kerry mentally to a life of deadly unforgiveness.

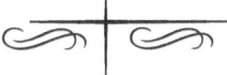

## THE END

# ABOUT THE AUTHOR

**Kimberley M. Byrd** is a native of Alabama where she happily lives with her husband LeCurtis.

*Son of the Forgiven* is her second novel following *Forbidden Fruit* and preceding *Vengeance Is Mine.* She also indulges in her first love, poetry by both writing and performing it. Kimberley is the founder of Poets' Square, an outdoor poetry event designed to showcase the talents of local poets.

Her most favorite thing to do outside of smiling is to motivate others. *10 Commandments for Dream Chasers: Dream Like God is Cheering for You* is her first non-fiction, which does just that. Developing the M.O.M. (Minister of Motivation) brand is her passion in which she breathes out motivation via different channels mostly with a minute of motivation, sixty seconds of life changing videos.

To keep up with her work, visit her website at:
www.WriteOnKim.com

## OTHER TITLES

**Forbidden Fruit**

**Son of the Forgiven**

**Vengeance Is Mine**

## SOCIAL MEDIA

**Facebook:** *Facebook.com/writeonkim*

**Twitter:** *@WriteOnKim*

**E-mail:** *PageTurner@WriteOnKim.com*

**Website:** *www.WriteOnKim.com*